Is Anybody There?

Vic Duggins

SAFE PASSAGE

Published by Safe Passage Publishing

For information, please contact:
Safe Passage Publishing
PO Box 11426
Knoxville TN 37939-1426
www.safepassagepublishing.com

Library of Congress Control Number: 2005908226

ISBN: 0-9772684-0-3

Printed in the United States of America

Table of Contents

This book is dedicated to all the angels
who have inspired us to take a closer look.

Acknowledgments

First and foremost this book is about love and I wish to acknowledge some of the many angels whose love has blessed my life and continues to light my way.

My joy, my wife, Gaily, who gave life and love back to me and in whose beautiful heart I have found my home.

Our soul mate, Nancy Ellen, once met always loved, and her John John whose generous and playful spirit makes a playground for us all.

My mother, Elizabeth, and her mother, Ira May, who loved me first and who set a standard of giving to which I still can only aspire.

My daughters, Lesley and Amy, my gentle teachers, who have loved me as only daughters can love their dad.

My mother-in-law, Georgia, and my stepsons, Brett and Derek, who took me in and made me their own.

Our spiritual collaborator and sweetheart, Margo, who coaxed my heart to open ever further and express itself.

Our babies, Ralph and Dianne, who first stood with Gail and me and have always celebrated our union.

My generous wordsmith, Polly, who introduced me to the tools and still instructs in their use.

And, finally, all the nameless and sometimes faceless angels who share their blessings often without our even noticing.

Throughout time
and yet beyond
Sweetness in the silence dwelling

No feature fixed
nor form imprisoned,
Spirit of my heart's desiring

Meetings without kiss
or parting
Presence shared that souls might touch

Light of love
always growing
Peace your gift, and you

Chapter One

No Feature Fixed

Darkness had long since embraced the city and finally even the diehard night people had deserted the streets of the harbor district. Distant thunder rumbled across the water as a squall blew in from the bay. Intermittent flashes of lightening extended illumination through the giant sixth-story window of the Spartan loft apartment revealing the solitary form sitting motionless before the blue glow of a computer screen.

The arched window stretching some ten feet from the floor to its apex was what had sold him on the apartment. Well, really, it had been just a large dusty attic in a two-hundred-year-old waterfront building erected as both office and warehouse for an import-export company. Tom Foster liked the building's history but he loved the window.

Since the breakup he had spent even more time than usual peering out on a world that seemed ever more remote. The window had become his favorite vantage point and the loft his headquarters for the countless hours he was logging as an unannounced occupant of late-night chat rooms.

Almost from the first he had realized that she had never intended to hurt him. In their own peculiar way they had really loved each other. And even though their personalities and disparate values had doomed their marriage from the beginning, the end, when it finally came, had left him bruised and alienated from both the world and himself.

Now the rain began to blow against his window bringing him at least partly out of the computer-induced stupor. How long had the screen been vacant of the incessant visual chatter that had occupied yet another evening and late night? Tom was about to slip silently from the current eavesdropping digital perch when a single letter appeared on his screen. Was it an “I” or was it the numeral “1”? A moment or two passed and then, very slowly at first, additional letters began to appear.

IS ANY BODY THERE?

Three minutes ago he was not only sleepy but nearly vegetative: how could he now be so alert? Almost without thinking, he very uncharacteristically began to strike his keys in response.

Yes, I suppose we're the last ones around and I was just about to leave.

DO YOU WANT TO VISIT OR DO YOU NEED TO GET SOME REST?

A few minutes ago I would have said "good night" but I think I might enjoy talking with you awhile.

WHY ARE YOU UP SO LATE?

Good question. I'm afraid that to the extent I know the answer it would be pretty long and boring.

MAKE YOU A DEAL. TAKE A RUN AT IT AND IF I GET BORED I'LL LET YOU KNOW.

Fair enough. But you must realize that if we knew each other this would be completely impossible instead of just extremely difficult. Even so, how do I begin?

Well, for starters, it probably goes back to the breakup of my former marriage and the fact that I don't seem to be myself these days.

WHO DO YOU SEEM TO BE?

Touché. But I think you know what I mean. I've lost my lust for life and I just want people to leave me alone.

IF SO, WHY DID YOU RESPOND TO MY INITIAL QUESTION?

That's another good question. Normally, or at least for the last several months, I have ducked every unnecessary contact with anybody and everybody. For some strange reason I felt like talking with you tonight. Go figure.

PERHAPS IT IS SIMPLY TIME. THINGS CHANGE WITH TIME AND HEALING IS THE

NATURAL ORDER OF THINGS. DON'T YOU AGREE?

I would like to think so, though I haven't held out much hope for that sort of thing lately. I guess I haven't been given to much coherent thought about anything now that I think about it.

MAYBE COHERENT THOUGHT IS OVERRATED. WHAT HAVE YOU BEEN THINKING OR FEELING THAT HAS KEPT YOU UP SO LATE AND HOW IS THIS RELATED TO THE BREAKUP YOU MENTIONED?

My thoughts have just swirled around in my head...kind of out of control, you know. And conscious thought, all conscious thought, is simply too painful to be endured. I lose myself by watching the world go by out my window or by spending hours "listening" to the conversation of others in chat rooms so that I can escape the pain of my own thinking or, really, of my situation. You see, since my former wife and I ended our marriage I feel so empty and, yes, so alone. True, we had reached the point where being together had become unbearable and yet now being alone seems almost as bad. I'm afraid things are too broken to be fixed. Do you know the expression about being "suspended between two worlds—one dead and the other powerless to be born"? My situation is even worse than that because I don't know what I want. I can't even imagine ever being happy again. God, I can't believe how pathetic this all looks in writing either!

GOOD THAT YOU SAID THAT INSTEAD OF ME! WRITING SEEMS TO BE A VERY EFFECTIVE MEANS OF PUTTING THINGS INTO PERSPECTIVE. YOU ARE OBVIOUSLY HEALTHIER THAN YOU HAVE GIVEN YOURSELF CREDIT FOR BEING OR YOU WOULD NOT HAVE RECOILED SO INSTINCTIVELY FROM DEPICTING YOURSELF IN SUCH "PATHETIC" TERMS. AND,

BY THE WAY, WHERE HAVE ALL YOUR FRIENDS BEEN DURING YOUR ORDEAL? WE ALL HAVE LONESOME VALLEYS WE HAVE TO WALK ALONE BUT SOMEWHERE OUT THERE THERE'S SUPPOSED TO BE SOME BUDDIES ON FUNK PATROL!

Strange that you should ask. I too have been troubled by the fact that all the people who have been most important in my life headed for the hills when the marriage started coming apart. You would think that I had developed a dreaded communicable disease. I'm sure I wouldn't have been very good company and that I've been more than a little crazy but the sudden and universal departures have definitely added to the pain.

SPRING CLEANING ALWAYS LEAVES THINGS BRIGHTER AND THE REMOVAL OF WHAT IS NO LONGER USEFUL MAKES ROOM FOR NEW AND MORE VALUABLE ADDITIONS TO

YOUR LIFE. PERHAPS YOU DON'T KNOW WHAT YOU WANT RIGHT NOW BECAUSE WHAT'S IN STORE FOR YOU IS BETTER THAN ANYTHING THAT YOU CAN, AT LEAST AT THIS POINT, IMAGINE. THE JOY THAT IS YOUR BIRTHRIGHT WILL FIND YOU WHEN YOU CAN HONESTLY EMBRACE ALL THE THINGS THAT HAVE VALUE FOR YOU. START ANYWHERE. START WITH THE SMALLEST AND SIMPLEST THINGS THAT YOU CARE ABOUT AND WOULD FEEL REGRET IF THEY WERE INJURED OR NO LONGER IN YOUR LIFE. FILL YOUR MINUTES, HOURS, AND DAYS WITH THESE THINGS AND WATCH YOUR THOUGHTS BECOME PLEASURABLE AGAIN. GIVING YOUR ATTENTION, YOUR ENERGY, INDEED YOUR LIFE TO THAT WHICH YOU TRULY VALUE IS ALWAYS ULTIMATELY A GIFT TO YOURSELF. LIVING THIS WAY PROTECTS YOU FROM BETRAYAL BY OTHERS BECAUSE YOU ACT OUT OF SELF-DIRECTED COMMITMENT RATHER THAN A SENSE OF DUTY OR A RESPONSE TO THE EXPECTATIONS OF OTHERS.

WELL I'LL STEP OFF MY SOAPBOX BEFORE I FALL OFF. LET'S JUST SAY THAT YOU'RE IN A LOT BETTER SHAPE THAN YOU REALIZE AND THAT YOU'RE IN A POSITION TO HELP YOURSELF OUT OF THIS HOLE IF YOU CAN BEGIN TO FOCUS ON WHAT YOU VALUE AND NOT ON WHAT HAS CAUSED YOU PAIN. DOES ANY OF THIS STRIKE A FAMILIAR NOTE?

ARE YOU STILL THERE OR DID I PUT YOU TO SLEEP?

Yes, I'm here and I'm anything *but* asleep! It's going to take some time to take all that in. But, for some reason, I feel better just sharing with you and feeling your concern. I've been able to share myself so freely because I don't know you and yet somehow I feel more comfortable with you than I have been with anybody in a long, long time. Do you think we could "talk" again sometime?

WELL WE DIDN'T PLAN THIS MEETING DID WE? A LOT OF VERY GOOD THINGS HAPPEN WITHOUT ANY PLANNING AT ALL. SO LET'S JUST SEE WHAT HAPPENS. I WISH YOU GREAT JOY. GOODNIGHT.

And just like that Tom's correspondent was gone. He stared at the empty screen for a few more minutes before becoming aware of the sweet breeze coming through the small window near his bed across the room. The rain had stopped but its lingering fragrance mixed with the faint scent of saltwater filled him with a gentle pleasure that was both pure and simple. Tom suspected that this reprieve from the turmoil of his recent past was only temporary but, nevertheless, too dear not to indulge. He accordingly made his way to bed and, bathed in the intoxicating early-morning air, slipped into the first truly peaceful sleep he had enjoyed in months.

Chapter Two

Cooper

Then it was morning. Morning, something Tom had not experienced during those months while under the influence of a near lethal emotional cocktail of one part pain, one part embarrassment, and two parts seething, slow-burn, all-consuming anger. Pain over having his deepest, truest self not only not valued but actually rejected and trashed like something of no worth or at least something that had outlived its usefulness. Embarrassment over having been judged so harshly and, perhaps most of all, over his own lack of judgment or self-respect in having invested so poorly that most valuable part of himself—even if its value was only to himself. And anger, my god, the anger over everything and everybody. Screw her and the horse she rode in on. In fact, damn every woman on the face of the planet. Were it possible he would have eagerly lived out his remaining days without female companionship and without ever again being told that he and his failings were the cause of some woman's unfulfilled dreams and unhappiness.

So why was this morning so different? Why was he up at the crack of dawn with this diffuse yet invigorating sense of excitement and expectation? Could this sudden change be the result of his late-night cyber chat with a faceless, nameless woman who had evaporated so quickly back into the blue glow from which she had mysteriously appeared? Tom's thoughts raced on but his spirit was curiously light.

Whatever the reason, here he was hitting the street at 6:00 a.m., as had been his habit in his former life. But something was definitely different. For while Tom had enjoyed a ten-year running love affair with the harbor district and especially its residents, this morning was total sensory overload. The sights and sounds and, yes, the smells of fresh brewed coffee, oven-warm bagels, the awakening open-air market featuring catches just off the boats, and the cut-flowers that were just that morning growing in long-row fields with their cousins.

Tom Foster was experiencing what it was to fall in love all over again. But had the district ever before been this tantalizingly alive for him—this compelling, this all encompassing? What had she said last night about embracing the smallest and simplest things? This must be what she had meant and surely this would be the easiest lesson he would ever undertake.

Tom ducked into Gus's. Yes, just Gus's. Apparently the old Greek had been inspired by the culinary nomenclature of the deep South as in Ma's, Eats, Billy Bob's, and Helma's. But "Bubba" Gus was not. His small diner-like establishment catered to virtually every ethnic taste represented in the district...including greasy cheeseburgers with thick sliced onion, grilled buns, and a mystery ingredient that left you coming back for more even when you had vowed your holiest promise never to put that concoction in your delicate stomach ever again.

The bald, sly-smiling head perched above a very ample, apron-draped body behind the counter took notice of Tom's arrival, "Tom you lose your watch or maybe you got a fever?"

Tom didn't even look up, "Hey, Gus. Why don't you mind your own business and fix me a bagel with lox and onion and pour me some of that poison you pass for coffee?"

"Hey Tommy! Leave my lover alone before I have to kick your sorry butt here in front of what you mistakenly refer to as your friends."

"Hey, Cooper. That's mean even for you. Somebody steal your comb and lipstick?" As with Gus, Tom didn't even look her way as he returned fire.

Cooper. Now there was a loose end if ever there was one. She was a thread that ran throughout Tom's life since he first arrived in the district to write for the *First Watch,* the Harbor's only local newspaper. She was the only person who had ever called him "Tommy", obviously to annoy him. It had worked and she had permanently adopted the practice.

She was in charge of circulation at the paper and managed the route men with an iron will, which had never been tested. Her unruly, short-chopped hair, total lack of make-up and perpetual bib overalls or slouchy cargo pants made her virtually invisible to both the men and women at the paper but, of course, for very different reasons.

Tom and Cooper had discovered each other at the paper's totally inane staff meetings. The meetings were a source of pride and entertainment for Preston Woods who owned and published the *First Watch* for his own amusement. Harold Woods, Preston's father, had amassed a fortune by inventing some sort of widget and selling the rights before the march of time and technology had rendered his invention totally useless. Harold's death was as untimely as his business timing was propitious and Preston was left with the proverbial shit-load of cash with which to buy himself all of the friends and toys that his wit and personality could never have provided with any amount of hard work and discipline.

To his credit Preston did love the district as much as Tom and, with his considerable resources, was one of the district's greatest champions and defenders; a job that required constant effort and vigilance as land developers circled the prime waterfront real estate like sharks with the smell of dollars in the water.

When Tom thought of business sharks it always conjured up the image of the "old man". The old man, his ex father-in-law, had also made a vast fortune by recognizing opportunity and having the balls and killer instinct to capitalize on his finds without regard to the price or consequences to be borne by others. His opening volley with Tom had been "Hell, Son, with your education and good looks and my connections and grit, my little girl will never want for anything!"

And with the *naivete'* of youth, Tom had underestimated and dismissed the clear and present danger and rushed in like Ringling's opening-act clown patrol. The inevitable closing act sounded something like "Tom Foster, you have foolishly rejected every opportunity Daddy has offered us and now you want to throw our lives away over that squalid little harbor district rag and the pitiful menagerie it serves. Chip Worthington is our friend at the club and the publisher of the most powerful paper in the city. He will do anything Daddy tells him to. For god's sake, if you must be a little writer man, at least do it for a big influential paper where we can have a little prestige."

Well, the die had been cast from the "gitgo" and when the dust had settled and Tom was left with only a bruised ego and a column and byline at the *First Watch*, he had been a shell shocked soldier without the benefit of a purple heart or post traumatic stress syndrome counseling.

It was during this time that his eyes had caught Cooper's across the room as the weekly staff meeting droned on. The instant recognition that there was indeed another human being in the world who could still smell bullshit was the basis for an unspoken bond and much conspiratorial mirth at Preston's expense as well as at the expense of all those colleagues with their noses so far up his ass that a proctologist would be required to untangle the mess.

Tom had easily fallen into Cooper's manner of relating to him with a feigned mocking tone that avoided at all cost any hint of affection. She was, however, perhaps the only one who didn't turn tail and run when his marriage hit the fan and his sense of self-worth hit the crapper. Her contribution was simply "Hang tough, Tommy, you ninety-pound weenie. Do whatever you have to do to survive the shitty mess you've made. It'll turn out a whole lot better than you deserve, you putz."

Chapter Three

Panic

By mid afternoon the magic was beginning to fade. What had she said and why had he listened to her in the first place? In fact, who the hell was she anyway and what kind of spell had he fallen under? Was anything changed from the day before—was he not the same guy with the same shitty luck and the same assholes for friends?

Just hours before, Tom had written his column with all the passion of an ardent lover. Words spilled onto the page and the drama and life force of the district came alive for his readers to share. The simplest details of the smallest lives had taken on a glow and a dignity that compelled rapt attention and genuine empathy. And then with the sinking finality of a crashing hard drive, the illusion and the writer crashed back to earth...back to reality.

Tom filed his column and left the office early. Too blue and agitated to return his calls and follow up on story leads, he walked the waterfront with a growing sense of panic. It had seemed so real, so right, and now it was falling apart and he was falling apart as well. The clear vision of the night before was disintegrating into fragments of ideas that now felt so foreign. But why had he, however temporarily, felt so good?

Like a user coming off a high, Tom was desperate to regain the euphoric optimism that had so recently rejuvenated his spirit. He had to reach his "supplier", his "dealer", his "source".

Christ, he didn't even know her name. She clearly represented a once-in-a-blue million shot in the dark and lightening was going to have to strike twice in the same place if he was to have any hope of making contact again.

Back in his attic apartment Tom fired up his Dell and returned to the chat room. It was book marked with his favorites so he was certain this was where the chance encounter had occurred. But he had monitored this location for months and only last night had he seen the uncharacteristic all-caps style of his mystery correspondent. Would it be months again or never? He had to try and this was the only way he knew how.

All night he kept his vigil without success. At first light he dropped exhausted onto his rumpled bed and fell immediately into a restless sleep that lasted until well past noon. After splashing water on his face, eating a can of room-temperature spaghettios, and attending to other body necessities, Tom returned to the task at hand.

Night after night, day after day, the mind-numbing routine continued. Then the door to the loft service elevator raised and Cooper walked in unannounced. “What in the name of all that is foul and unholy have you done, Tommy?!” The apartment was a wreck and it looked good in comparison with Tom. “Preston has been trying to call you for days and all he has been getting is a busy signal. Have you been off this machine of Satan even once in the past two weeks? Boy is he pissed! Tommy where have you been and what the hell have you been doing? I know you and Preston have this harbor district crusade thing going but not even you can get away with something like this, cowboy. Get you sorry ass into the shower while I make some industrial strength coffee. Then you have some ‘splaning to do, Lucy!’”

Two hours later, a somewhat restored if not repentant Tom finished his tale of woe as a totally incredulous Cooper shook her head and sighed.

“You’re chasing a ghost, Tommy, and what makes you think this Wonder Woman of Cyberspace knows anything more about anything than any of the rest of us? I’ve got to tell you that to me this all seems like an elaborate excuse for you to crawl back up here in your damn dirty cocoon and hide from the world again and this shit has got to stop, Bucko.”

“You can’t begin to know how she made me feel, Coup. Even if for only a matter of hours, it was really good to be alive again. But the words are gone and maybe it was more than just the words, I don’t know. I do know there’s a lot I want to ask her and I want that feeling back...more than anything...more than everything.”

"Well, ok, you pathetic piece of shit. Let me see if I can help. But your sorry butt is going back to work 'cause I ain't running no stinking soup kitchen and there's a real question as to whether you even have a job to go to."

Chapter Four

The Search

By the time Tom arrived at the office, Cooper had already smoothed the way with Preston and had disappeared saying something about needing some expertise before this thing got totally out of hand.

Preston looked over the top of his reading glasses as Tom entered the publisher's expensively appointed office designed to recreate the flavor of the nineteenth century—complete with a mahogany roll-top and dark hardwood wainscoting.

"I don't pay you to sit on your ass at home, Tom."

"You don't pay me enough for cab fare home, you tightwad. Did you miss me?"

"Probably not as much as those two or three readers you pay to call me and brag on your column. Sounds like you've got yourself even more screwed up than you were before, Buddy, and, believe me, that's really saying something. Do you just sit around thinking up these damn crazy ideas? Go get yourself laid or get a hobby. Your current choices are totally self destructive you know."

"Not that its any of your damn business, but, yes, you're probably pretty much right on all counts and, now that you mention it, I have been having wet dreams about bowling."

"Get the hell out of my office and let the few of us who have some claim to sanity get back to work. You're worthless and I don't know why I let you hang around. Make sure this crisis *de jour* doesn't last as long as the last one. If you're not dazzling me with your horseshit prose in, say, ninety days, I will be forced to look for some other sucker with an English degree to sit at your desk and provide me with an excuse for migraines."

Cooper was at Tom's desk with her feet propped up when Tom emerged from Preston's inner sanctum. He didn't recognize the studious looking little fellow sitting with her. Surely if they had met before Tom would have remembered the thick, round coke-bottle glasses and the carrot orange hair.

"Tommy, meet Sidney. You don't know him of course because Sid actually does something constructive around here. In fact, if it weren't for Sid's expertise all these newsroom monitors, keyboards, and CPU's would be little more than expensive paperweights. Out of the goodness of his heart and in return for my discretion regarding some of Sid's improprieties with respect to certain sensitive company equipment, Sid is going to help you track down Cyber Lady. Then maybe we can all get on with our lives of quiet desperation."

"Hear you're looking for some broad who yanked your chain on the net." So clearly Ole Sidney was a poet at heart but, at this point, Tom was too desperate to be choosy about his allies.

"Something like that. I'm afraid I don't have much to go on. I not only don't know her name, I can't really say that I know anything about her," Tom sheepishly admitted.

"Well I sure as hell would like to know what she said to you that's got you so wired. In the meantime, I'll settle for the date and time the two of you had your little chat-room *rendezvous.*" Sid was clearly down to business.

"That may be a problem. So much time has gone by and most of it with me in a stupor."

"With your head up your ass you mean," Cooper corrected. "We can figure this out, Sid. It was the night before Tommy Boy wrote the only decent column he's come up with since his previous misadventure with a female. It's truly a miracle that the lad hasn't just hung it up. Yet here he is pestering the hound out of every living soul he knows trying to locate yet another broad who didn't even care enough about him to give him her number. Come on Genius, let's look up the date of your fucking masterpiece."

Over the next few days Tom came to understand that for all the legitimate endeavors Sidney undertook for the *First Watch* during regular working hours, Sidney was an after-hours impresario of digital skullduggery. Furthermore, according to Sidney, everything that had ever appeared on Tom's monitor was still preserved in some form or other in his CPU's memory—even material that had not been intentionally saved or, more astonishing yet, even material which had not been generated by Tom himself. Most of the technical jargon went straight over Tom's head but at one point his ears perked up again when Sidney observed, "...mind you I could sure enough do it if I had the equipment and software, but I may need one of my nameless co-conspirators over at NSA to actually track down her address if we don't get enough data from your chat-room conversation."

"Ah, excuse me," Tom was now fully engaged in the dialog, "I don't wish to split legal hairs here but I have a definite aversion to prison showers. Maybe we should give my chat-room monitoring plan a few more days to work.

You're a real *mensch* there Sidney and the next time I need a second-story man you'll be at the top of my list. Hell, you'll be on my speed dial."

Sidney seemed genuinely disappointed to pass up the challenge but he left more or less agreeably and when he was out of sight, "Cooper, you are truly a wild woman, over the top, out of control and out of sight! What in the world were you thinking?"

As usual Cooper only shook her head and muttered under her breath as she too walked away, "Tommy, you're a 24-karat pussy. I don't know why I even try."

Tom's exit through the reception area brought flirtatious taunts and overtures from the gaggle of receptionists, clerks, and secretaries who perched high on their stiletto heels and, with their too skimpy attire and too generous appendages, circled any unattended male who appeared to be well-heeled or at least handsome enough to provide entertainment until the real thing came along. Tom's smile was friendly but inside he observed to himself, "Why are the available, even eager, ones always the ones that hold no interest? And why are the good ones so damn much trouble? Must the best fruit always hang on the highest branches?"

Chapter Five

A Closer Look

Emerging from *First Watch*, Tom was confronted by a pouring rain that perfectly matched his dark mood. As was his custom, he walked anyway and by the time he reached the Southern Cross Mercantile building he was soaked to the bone. Inside he rejected the mechanics of the freight elevator and took the dimly lit but unusually wide stairway to the sixth floor.

Rain beat hard against his huge arched window and his apartment seemed unbearably empty. Maybe he ought to get a cat—something to come home to. Home indeed. Tom could scarcely recall the feeling of home. He was raised as an only child and both of his parents had died so long ago that the memories had lost their emotional juice and seemed almost as sterile as the old black and white photos that bore fading witness to what had once been.

His ex, even though she had made a home, it wasn't his home. There had been no place there for who he was and he had no stomach for even trying to become the person who would have fit her expectations.

Still, there it was. This vague longing for something he had probably never experienced; something that seemed an echo of a half-conscious impression of home.

He hadn't eaten all day except for a stale, rubbery bagel that he washed down with some god-awful coffee that morning. He couldn't face another can of spaghettios and he didn't have the heart to go back out or prepare something in. Two handfuls of peanuts washed down with some really suspect orange juice and Tom collapsed on top of his equally suspect bed linens. He was wounded but numb and all he wanted, desperately wanted, was sleep, not restful sleep but escape sleep. He was just soul weary of the whole damn thing including himself, maybe especially himself.

Darkness when it came was ice cold, bone-chilling, black water and he was running out of breath. But the more he struggled to move toward the faint light that he took for the surface, the heavier his arms and legs became. He was not moving at all. Then just as his fear and exhaustion merged into a final profound resignation, he felt gentle hands guiding his now still body toward the light.

He awoke with a start, aware of the morning sun on his sweat-beaded face. His tee was damp around the collar and he could almost believe it was saltwater from the black depths of his dream.

The numbness was still there but the angst and agitation had passed. For the first time since "Day One", what Tom had by now named his fleeting post-chat room euphoric episode, he was experiencing a calm that allowed him to think quietly instead of bouncing off every surface at once with a wounded bull mentality that had raged out of control.

In this more tranquil state Tom now reverted to his old habit of playing back situations and bits of dialog that his subconscious had filed away for a closer look when he was ready to truly listen. What he "heard" now was Sidney saying something about retrieving enough data from the chat with Cyber Lady. Of course! If was still stored in the computer's memory, it was still stored in his subconscious memory as well!

Tom grabbed his reporter's notebook off the crate that served as a bedside table. What had she said? That he was better off than he realized. And she had indicated that the way out of his malaise was to focus on the little things that really mattered to him. But here he was stumped. Why had that focus or perspective been so easy on Day One and so seemingly impossible ever since?

As the morning slipped by Tom filled his notebook with recollected bits and pieces of his fateful cyber chat and increasingly interspersed his own thoughts and questions. The answer to his first question seemed to be taking shape in his mind. His perspective on Day One was a natural outgrowth of the vision that Cyber Lady had shared with him—a kind of freebie. The task she had set for him was, however, going to involve real effort on his part if he were to succeed, a kind of spiritual discipline he supposed. For he realized that he had not yet taken the time to reflect on what really held value for him at this point. How curious that he didn't have a ready answer for such a fundamental question.

Now the writing stopped and the investigative reporter instincts gave way to a reflective reverie that slowed Tom's breathing and relaxed his tense, preoccupied body and mind. What did have real value in his life? Had he ever at any point in his life given this most basic of questions any consideration at all? Was it possible that he had lived for decades on this planet without any conscious direction? If so, he must have had a defective autopilot that had steered him into such troubled waters. Or was it his autopilot that had brought him to this point of self-awareness?

What did he care about so much that he wished to see it protected? Certainly the Harbor District and its rich tapestry of ethnicity and diverse activity qualified. Then there was the

First Watch that served as advocate, chronicler, and protector of the district. And, strange as it might seem, there was Cooper. How had she managed to make the list without his even taking notice of her expanding presence in his life?

"Well," he reasoned, "she was really more like an intruding, irritating grain of sand in the soft center of an oyster." Where had that image come from? Tom uncomfortably noted that he didn't care to pursue that metaphor any further.

And how could the list of things he valued be so embarrassingly small? What kind of moron lived willingly in such a diminutive personal world as to have resonated with so few treasures? Not a comforting thought at all!

Then came the bruising realization that far from nurturing that which had value for him, however small the list, he had been guilty of self-centered neglect. And, in the case of Cooper, his manner had been an annoyed lack of appreciation for her uninvited, but nonetheless sincere, efforts on his behalf.

This last realization ached in his heart in spite of his feeble attempts at rationalization. With a value list so small, how could he have screwed up so badly?

Maybe it was stabbing hunger or the equally painful self-knowledge that was emerging; maybe it was something else. Whatever the reason, Tom suddenly exited his meditation and looked around the now darkened room. He had lost the whole afternoon in this disturbing, dreamlike state of altered consciousness and what had felt like suspended time and space had obviously consumed more time than he could imagine possible.

While rummaging in the fridge, Tom's peripheral vision registered a familiar image across the room. There on his monitor, in all caps, was the simple, illusive question...

IS ANY BODY THERE?

Chapter Six

Wants and Needs

At first it didn't seem real, didn't seem possible. After all this time and effort, there it was, unbidden, enigmatic, and ephemeral. Tom shook off the paralysis of surprise and rushed to his keyboard.

Where have you been? I have needed you so badly but I didn't know how to find you. For God's sake, I have been in a total panic. I don't even know your name.

UNLESS YOU KNOW MY HEART, MY NAME IS MEANINGLESS. I AM PLEASED TO BE WITH YOU AGAIN. WHY THE PANIC?

The day after we first met, what I have come to call "Day One," I came alive again, maybe totally alive for the first time ever. It was sensory overload and my heart was bursting with joy. I wrote the best column I had ever written and then, just like that, it all started slipping away.

I think I understand now that I was running on the euphoria of my time with you and that it couldn't last unless we were together on an ongoing basis so that I could learn from you and touch you.

I'M AFRAID THAT IS QUITE IMPOSSIBLE. WHAT DO YOU FEEL YOU HAVE LEARNED FROM ME THAT IS OF SUCH VALUE THAT YOU HAVE FOCUSED SO MUCH ATTENTION ON CONTACTING ME AGAIN?

Well, for starters, I have realized that there are very few things that I truly value in this world and that I have neglected even these.

LET ME ASSURE YOU THAT TO KNOW LOVE IS TO KNOW EVERYTHING OF VALUE. YOUR HEART IS YOUR COMPASS. IT WAS DESIGNED BY LOVE TO GUIDE YOU BACK TO THE LOVE FROM WHICH YOU CAME. YOU CANNOT BECOME LOST FOR YOU ARE ALWAYS THERE. YOU CAN ONLY FORGET HOW TO SEE. SEE WITH YOUR HEART, TOM. FEEL EVERYTHING AROUND YOU AND REMEMBER. YOU ARE AT ONCE MUCH LARGER AND MUCH SMALLER THAN YOU CAN IMAGINE. BUT SUCH CONSIDERATIONS ARE POINTLESS AS LOVE VALUES THE LARGEST AND THE SMALLEST, THE STRONGEST AND THE WEAKEST AS ONE. LOVE KNOWS ITS OWN AND THEREIN LIES YOUR BIRTHRIGHT.

See, there you go again. Do you have any concept of how long it will take me to figure out all by myself what you have just said—even if I could remember it? I need your help. I need you.

ALL THAT YOU NEED IS TO KNOW WHAT LIES WITHIN YOU, TOM. ALL WISDOM IS ACCESSIBLE TO YOUR HEART. AND KNOW THIS, WE ARE NEVER ALONE. YOU WILL NEED TO LEARN TO BE VERY STILL BEFORE YOU CAN DISCERN THE VOICES OF THOSE WHO CONSTANTLY SURROUND YOU WITH LOVE AND WHO STAND READY TO GUIDE YOU TOWARD YOUR HEART'S OWN WISDOM AND PATH. BE CONTENT NOW TO FOCUS ON AND NURTURE THAT WHICH YOU KNOW AND WATCH IT EXPAND AS IF BY MAGIC. THERE IS A VAST DIFFERENCE BETWEEN WHAT WE WANT AND WHAT WE NEED. WANTS ARE PRODUCTS OF OUR EGOS AND RARELY SATISFY THE HEART. NEEDS, ON THE OTHER HAND, HAVE ALREADY BEEN SATISFIED BY OUR CREATOR AND THEREFORE HAVE LITTLE MEANING OTHER THAN INSTRUCTION.

YOU ARE SO BLESSED. YOU HAVE ALREADY BEEN GIVEN EVERYTHING OF VALUE. LISTEN TO YOUR HEART AND SEE. YOU ARE PERFECTLY SAFE IN A UNIVERSE OF UNIMAGINABLE TREASURES. AND, WHAT IS MORE, YOU HAVE BEEN GIVEN THE GIFT OF CO-CREATION TO EXPAND THAT UNIVERSE. WAKE UP, TOM, AND ENJOY YOUR GIFTS. I LOVE YOU.

Wait, don't leave again. I haven't told you how much I appreciate what you have shared with me. I have so many more questions. How can I reach you?

There was no response. His teacher was either gone or not responding. Tom was both sad and exhilarated. He must not lose this feeling again. He knew he had work to do.

Chapter Seven

Pete

Tom's unexpected arrival at *First Watch* the next morning caused something of a stir in the corridors. And around the water coolers gossip spread that the prodigal had returned and that there was a discernable change in his countenance.

Before long Preston stuck his head into Tom's cubical, "Back so soon this time? Have you wooed and won Cyber Lady or did you just drop by to water your plants?"

"Preston you have a gift, Old Chum. I'll bet you sour milk when you walk by."

"What do you know of milk, Longfellow? I thought you drank printers' ink and picked your teeth with a quill."

"Jesus, Preston, that's lame even for you. Have you seen Cooper this morning?"

Tom found Cooper on the loading dock supervising the arrival of yesterday's returns, "Hey Coup, got a minute?"

She eyed Tom cautiously, "Tommy, I don't have time for your crap. I realize now that I never did, but I'm a slow learner."

"Not as slow as me, kiddo. Please just a minute, then I'll disappear—for good if you like."

When they reached one of the outdoor concrete picnic tables provided for the hourly workers' lunch breaks, she faced him and frowned, "What's so damn important? Do you need another favor in your holy quest for your love in cyber space? Need someone to hold your hand while you screw up your pathetic little life?"

"I know I deserve that. I've been a real jerk. All I want now is to apologize for not being, or at least, not showing that I'm grateful. You've been great, a real friend. I don't know why. Hell, I don't know anything about you and I'm sorry for that too. If I hadn't had my head up my ass, I might have thought to ask how you were doin' now and then. Might have asked if there was anything I could do for you instead of thinking only about myself. I wish I had at least asked your last name."

At that, Cooper held up her hand in a "stop" gesture and grinned from ear to ear. "Tommy, my name, you really want to know my last name. Coming from you, that's the nicest thing anyone has ever said to me. Tommy asked my name. Well I'll be damned. There may be hope for you yet, cowboy!" She paused, looked thoughtful for a moment, and then, "Tell you what, Tommy, I've got to get back to work, but you meet me Saturday morning at Gus's—let's say six sharp. Wear jeans and sneakers but bring shorts or swim trunks. I'll not only tell you my name, I'll show you who I am."

She was up and gone in one swift motion and Tom realized that he was already filled with anticipation and maybe some other emotion that was less familiar.

Saturday dawned bright and clear with a breeze that ruffled your hair and lightened your step. Gus only smiled and pointed toward

Cooper's usual booth in the back corner and allowed Tom to pass the front counter and display case without further harassment.

"It's Cooper. You've always known my last name, dimwit. It's my first name that has eluded you. I hope you're in the mood for a tall stack with boysenberries and links 'cause that's what I ordered and what you're gettin'."

"Are you always this bossy in the morning? And, just for the record, what's your first name and why don't you use it?" Tom was just settling into his end of her booth and thinking that he had never sat there before—had never seen anybody sit there.

"I don't use it because it's very special to me and I'm very careful about who I share my special things with. You know that thing about not casting your pearls before swine. Well, I've always felt that way. My name is Emily Cathlene

Cooper. Emily, for my grandmother who helped raise me and, Cathlene, for my mother who died much too young. These names are treasures to me and I would very much appreciate you're keeping them to yourself. OK?"

Tom hesitated before answering, "It's a beautiful name, old and charming like fine bone china. And, of course, I will keep it to myself. Thank you for entrusting your treasure with me. But you'll be eating all the sausage or suffering my gas as a consequence of not consulting me before ordering."

Back on the street with loosened belts and sticky chins, Cooper ushered Tom to her "car".

"You're kidding me! This '45 woodie is yours? I've seen it around but I had no idea. Cooper, you're a woman of impeccable taste!"

He threw his gym bag in the back and, as they took the coast road south, he admired the carefully maintained interior. Not a prissy restored for show but a lovingly maintained out of appreciation kind of vehicle that clearly was used and not mollycoddled.

“Where are you taking me, oh mysterious one? You know I’ve been thinking that I don’t have a clue as to how you spend your time away from *First Watch*. I don’t believe anyone does.”

“Just shut your yap and pay attention, girly mon. You just might learn something that you didn’t come across at that hoity-toity Ivy League rip-off you attended.” This last was clearly all tease and had none of the sarcastic tone that had characterized much of their customary *repartee*’.

The ocean appeared and reappeared to their left for the next half-hour or so and then

Cooper started to slow as they approached a sun-bleached old board sign that said simply “Pete’s Marina”.

“This Pete sure isn’t going to attract much business with that sign. You can barely read its faded letters.”

Cooper smiled a knowing glance his way, “Pete’s not looking for business. He likes things pretty much just the way they are. In fact, he may kick your butt in the water. He doesn’t care much for strangers.”

They wound their way down a sandy lane that was little more than a path through the sea oats until a quaint little marina came into view at the bottom of the hill. It was sheltered by similar hills on three sides and was the picture of serenity.

Tom observed that even from some distance it was clear that all of the vessels in the marina were vintage craft and yet all were in remarkably good repair. It looked like the set of a movie or the subject of some romantic seascape.

As they approached the weathered docks, an antique looking teak schooner was just slipping her mooring. An elderly gentleman was gliding over her decks adjusting lines and readying the canvas for a late morning sail.

"That's Oliver Newton," said Cooper. "Don't let his distinguished gray fool you, he's as quick and nimble as a cat. And although he's not given to many words, he's probably the best sailor on the coast."

Tom looked on with obvious awe. "He has the grace of a Tai Chi master in a Beijing park. His Zen energy makes me wish I knew more about boats and sailing. Just watching yacht racing on T.V., I have never before realized there could be so much poetry involved in piloting a boat."

"Why, Tommy, I do believe you're recapturing your appreciation for life outside that warped, overworked head of yours. This outing may prove to be a good idea after all."

As they left the woodie, Cooper threw a duffle bag over her shoulder and handed Tom a large wicker picnic basket to carry along with his gym bag. He followed her down to the middle dock and out to the end slip where she boarded a beautiful sloop. The hull was deep blue and white. All of the topside wood was in perfect condition and all of the brass work was polished and gleaming in the sun. Neatly painted on the stern in navy letters was "Cathlene's Dream."

"Mom always wanted her own boat but never realized her dream. Whenever I take the

Cathlene out, it's part for Mom and part for me. I feel Mom sailing with me and whenever I sleep onboard I always dream of her." A pause and then, "This is another treasure, Tommy. Please let's keep it to ourselves."

Cooper took her duffle bag and the picnic basket below while Tom inspected things topside. In a few minutes Cooper appeared at the top of the companionway. Tom gasped and put a hand on the gunwale to steady himself. She was wearing tan short shorts with a white T-shirt. For the first time ever, Tom became aware of her remarkable figure. Her tan shapely arms and legs, her tiny waist that accentuated her attractively proportioned torso, made an impression of natural beauty that at once left him breathless and yet filled to overflowing with something more precious than breath. Her smile was mocking and warm as Tom continued to struggle for breath. The baggy, boyish

Cooper was gone and the vision that stood before him had left him speechless.

"Cat got your tongue, Preppy? Why don't you go below and change. It's time we were shoving off."

When Tom emerged on deck he felt pale and awkward in his swim trunks. He was ready to duck back below when he caught sight of the biggest, darkest, most imposing mountain of a man he had ever encountered coming toward them across the dock.

"Hi, Pete. This is Tommy. He's new around here."

Tom remembered what Cooper had said about Pete not taking kindly to strangers and something else about being kicked overboard. "Oh shit," he thought, "I'm about to become shark bait right here in front of Cooper."

Cooper threw her arms around the big man's neck in a long, warm hug and then woolied his thick black beard with her knuckles. "Be nice, Pete, he's just a little pale landlubber and, as you can see, he's quite harmless."

Tom didn't know whether to be insulted or grateful. Then a gleam was clearly visible in Pete's deep-set, dark eyes and a grin, a very warm grin, started to form around his lips, "Welcome, Son, we've been expecting you."

"Hey, you two get acquainted for a minute. I forgot something in the car," laughed Cooper as she jumped from the stern to the dock.

When she was out of earshot, Pete turned to Tom, "Hope you understand what's going on here. This is the first time that little girl has ever brought anyone here to sail. You may get some stares around here, boy, don't pay it any mind. Everyone here has known her all of her life and they're pretty curious. You two have a good sail."

With that he was gone. No questions. No small talk. Pete had done his thing and he was leaving the couple to do theirs.

Chapter Eight

Free as the Wind

Cathlene's Dream cleared the cove and moved into blue water. Tom had leaned back against the transom and watched as Cooper alternated between the helm and tending the sails. The sun was bright overhead in an incredibly blue sky adorned with generous white clouds that moved with the stiff breeze. The admixture of sun sear and wind on his arms and legs coupled with the peaceful sounds of the wop of the sail as the boat came about and the incessant gurgle of the water slipping along the hull created a spell that was curiously both exhilarating and serene. Tom realized that it had been a very, very long time since he had been so relaxed and had experienced—what was it, yes, he had almost forgotten the sensation—fun. Pure, unadulterated fun!

Now with Cooper's back to him, he could see the design on the back of her tee. It was a blue outline of a sailboat with the caption "Free as the Wind" and, with the wind in her hair, he was acutely aware that the choppy style that had seemed unruly at the office was perfectly suited to this environment. In fact, he laughed to himself as he imagined any of those coiffed females back at *First Watch* attempting to cope with this situation. "Dame overboard! Somebody fetch the sharks!"

The afternoon sped by amid laughter, apples and bananas, and lots of iced tea. Tom could not get his fill of Cooper's tea. She had tenderness in her voice as she shared how her mother had taught her the tea secrets that her mother had learned from Cooper's grandmother long before Cooper was born. Tea never goes in anything but glass. It must never be bruised by placing the bags in boiling water. And on and on went the instruction that made the O'Malley women as famous for their tea as they were for their infamous ancestry of female pirates.

As the sun approached the horizon, Cooper eased the boat into a quiet cove, struck the main sail, and dropped anchor. For the first time, it occurred to Tom that this wasn't just an afternoon outing and he hoped he had thought to include a toothbrush in his ditty bag. As adventures go, an outing with Cooper was definitely getting high marks. In fact, prospects seemed to be favoring a perfect ten.

The cove had not been visible to Tom and could be detected only by a sailor who ventured so close to shore as to risk running aground on a sand bar or, worse, striking one of the rocks that broke the surface some 200 meters out. Having once negotiated the narrow cutback entrance, the sheltered water was wide and deep and surrounded by hills covered with dense vegetation. This had to be a favorite destination for Cooper, the kind of secret that seemed to play such an important role both in her personality and in her clandestine lifestyle.

"Well, Tommy Boy, its time for a swim so's I'm not haunted by your sweaty pits all night." And before Tom realized what was happening, off went the tee, the shorts, and the panties--the gorgeous tan body, sans tan lines, disappeared over the side and made a smooth entrance into the tranquil water. "Come on, girly mon, nothin' in here but gators and sharks and your skinny ass wouldn't interest either one."

If Tom's polite body looked pale, it was nothing compared to the pasty white that emerged as he dropped his trunks and made a mighty splash into the water butt first. The chill was something of a surprise and Tom was aware of his privates virtually disappearing into a tiny knot. Oh well, at least he wouldn't be embarrassed by an all too obvious demonstration of his excitement when they got back on board.

"It's too damn cold! How can it be so warm up there and like ice down here?" Tom complained. He splashed water in Cooper's face and immediately realized the error of his ways. She disappeared beneath the water and the next thing Tom knew a hand from behind him was pushing his head down as he sputtered a protest that was lost in bubbles.

By the time he had regained his composure if not his dignity, Cooper had climbed up the boarding ladder and stepped over the transom. She disappeared below deck and reappeared with one towel wrapped around her slender frame and tossed a second one to Tom as he too came aboard, “Here, cry baby, dry yourself off while I rustle up some grub. When you’re dry, you can uncork one of those bottles of red. The cork screw is in the basket with the wine.”

As they settled into the sandwiches and pasta salad that Cooper had prepared before daylight that morning, Tom remembered that stale dog food would taste like a feast in the outdoors, especially after a busy day. This, on the other hand, was definitely not dog food and the flavor was more intoxicating than the wine.

After several unusually large mouth fulls, Cooper broke the silence, “What did you think of Pete?”

“To be perfectly honest, he scared the crap out of me at first. I thought I was about to meet my maker in a most disagreeable manner.

Normally in a situation like that I stop and ask myself what Blackbeard would do. In this case I was too afraid and, luckily, I spotted the twinkle in his eye before I had an accident in my pants."

"What does asking about Blackbeard tell you? Do you ever get any really good strategy that way?"

"It isn't about strategy. Asking the question moves me from the position of victim to a place where I'm the one in charge. I'm the one who is contemplating my next lethal move to slay the dragon and win the lady."

"My hero," she sighed. Then with a twinkle in her own eyes that seemed very familiar, she confessed, "The reason I asked is that Pete's my father, Tommy. I know it was rude of me not to have told you sooner but I so wanted the two of you to judge the cut of each other's jibs before I put in my two cents worth.

Please don't be angry; I know Pete can be very intimidating. I'm glad you recognized his twinkle for yourself 'cause he's really a teddy bear who wouldn't harm anything or anyone unless he was defending something he loves from harm. Then you don't want to be on the same planet with him!"

"Hard to believe that little ole you came from someone as massive as Pete" replied Tom. "And, no, I'm not upset. If I were, you'd tell Pete and I'd be right back where I started asking for advice from Blackbeard. But, speaking of Pete, just how much pain am I in for if I keep his little girl out all night?"

"First of all, big boy, you're not keeping me out. I'm keeping you out and, unlike you, Pete knows me well enough to know that. Secondly, Pete and I have always had each other's back and have respected each other's privacy. It's hard to put into words but I guess you'd have to say that for the last twenty-some years we've been all each other's got. I'm proud to be his daughter but it's more than that. We're each other's best friend and we have real joy and respect in each other's lives. Do you understand what I'm trying to explain?"

"I understand that you're a very remarkable person and that Pete is truly blessed. When you said that you were going to show me who you are this weekend, I had no idea what an extraordinary person I have been working with these last few years. I really have had my head up my ass, haven't I?"

"Tommy, you've been through a lot. You've handled your pain without shitting on anyone else and when you've been crazy you've done your thing without taking out ads and trying to make your problems a matter of public record. You're a stand-up guy in my book. But what I really want to understand is what's up with this cyber space romance of yours. Please tell me about her so I can make some kind of sense out of this thing."

They weren't going anywhere. There was no schedule. No distractions. Only each other and a sky that was starting to fill with stars. So, with a deep breath, Tom started at the beginning and once again shared his whole experience with the only person on earth who really wanted to understand. Who really cared.

She had listened without comment or interruption of any kind. When he ran out of words, it was quiet for a long time. Only the gentle creaking of the boat and the distant undulating drone of insects. No, there was more. There was the sound of breathing and the indefinable sound of the universe.

Finally, she spoke, "Tommy, maybe I'm missing something here but I'm really confused.

I have listened very carefully this time and I have yet to hear anything that gives this person any humanity. You don't know her name. You don't know where she lives or what she looks like. As far as I can tell, you don't even know if you're communicating with a female instead of a male. Hell, Tommy, for all you know, you may be "talking" to a ghost or an alien from outer space or another dimension. How can you become so obsessed with someone without a body?"

This time the silence was deafening. Tom was stunned as her words, her observations, slowly sunk in. Was he like a dog chasing a car down the block? What would he do if he caught up with his prey? What was he chasing and why? Yet, while he could acknowledge the logic of Cooper's inquiries, they seemed to leave him more confused than ever and even strangely defensive. "Coup, I hear what you're saying.

Can we leave it at that for now? I just can't talk about this anymore tonight. Understand?"

She heard the confusion in his voice and half saw the pain in his face reflected in the dim light coming from the cabin below. "Sure, baby, it's no biggie. I've got some sleeping bags stowed around here someplace, let's put them down on the bow and sleep under the stars."

In the shelter of the hidden cove, all running and anchor lights extinguished, the couple cuddled in the deep velvet darkness of the mild night. They could feel each little catch of breath as a shooting star traced its patch across the cosmos. They breathed in unison and perhaps shared the same dream.

Chapter Nine

What Would Blackbeard Do?

One of nature's naughty tricks is to speed up time when we're really having fun and to slow things down to excruciating lengths when we're most ready to move on. True to form, the weekend outing was all too soon over and *Cathlene's Dream* was approaching the marina under full sail.

The morning swim, the laughter, the eggs and coffee complimented by the blueberry muffins Cooper had smuggled out of Gus's the morning before and tucked into the picnic basket when Tom wasn't looking, everything had been perfect. But now their happiness was tinged with the regret of going back to the city. No, it was what was ending not what was ahead that seemed to be robbing the moment of some of its joy.

As they neared the appointed slip, a rumpled little man with big bushy eyebrows just visible beneath his slouchy seaman's hat reached to secure their mooring lines, "Did you have a good sail, Miss Emily?"

"Yes, Campy. Good of you to ask. Campy, this is my friend, Tommy."

"I remember, Miss Emily, I'll take good care of your friend" the wizened old fellow secured the lines without looking up or making eye contact and disappeared down the dock.

Cooper acknowledged the question in Tom's eyes, "Campy is a little slow and a whole lot shy. He has been with Pete forever and had a hand in raising me when Pete was out of his mind with grief over Mom's passing. He knew grandmother from the time she came to look in on Pete and he's always chosen to call me by her name."

"Does he live here or work here?"

"Both, actually. That's Campy's houseboat tied up over there by itself. He lives there with Caroline, his calico cat. Hard to say which is older, they are both permanent residents. Pete and Campy built the houseboat before Pete began work on the marina. Campy also helped build the little stone cottage for my parents up on the side of the hill. While Mom was living she always cooked supper for both of them and they would sit on the side porch and watch the sun set beyond the cove. Now Pete cooks supper and Campy does the dishes. So, you see, Campy and Caroline are our adopted family. They're a part of this place like Mom. No one ever really leaves the cove."

By the time all of the onboard gear was stowed, the hatches secured, and the bags and basket were being ferried toward the woodie, Pete was waiting at the end of the dock, "Had you some good weather. Is Tom going to make a sailor?"

"He'll be crewing with the best of 'em in no time. Wouldn't hurt if you wanted to share some of that unfathomable seamanship that you're always spouting, though. If I had to live through it, he shouldn't be spared either," Cooper teased.

"By the way, that Preston fellow at the paper called while you were out. Asked if you knew how he could catch up with Tom. I just said you weren't here and he said if I heard from you to say it was real important that he find Tom right away. Didn't offer any real skinny and was kinda short to tell it true," Pete's opinion was coming through.

"Thanks, Pete. I haven't turned on my cell all weekend. Haven't missed it either. Why don't you two say your goodbyes while I put this stuff in the woodie and see if I can get Preston on the horn? This is a magical place you have here. Thanks for letting a landlubber stranger invade your world."

"Any time Sissy wants to bring you back, you'll be welcome. Glad you like the place but I'd be much obliged if you'd just keep it to yourself. The fewer people who know about us the better I like it."

"Pete's not much of a Dale Carnegie fan," laughed Cooper, "but then we just put up with him the way he is. Can't teach an old dog, even an old sea dog, you know."

Tom had not been able to acquire a cell signal within the confines of the cove, so when Cooper reached the woodie they left for the coast road wondering what had prompted Preston to call with such urgency. When Tom did get through, Preston was out of the office and was not available by his mobile number. There was nothing left to do but keep driving and keep trying not to acknowledge the sense of foreboding they both felt.

"Coup, this weekend. I can't find words."

"That's a good thing, preppy, I'd be disappointed if you could. Writer or not, there are some things that are best left unsaid. It's kind of like music. The rests are as important as the notes. As good as you are with words, I am most impressed when you choose to remain silent."

That's just what they did the rest of the way back. It was a wonderful, richly intimate silence that was much more than just being quiet alone could ever be.

Cooper dropped Tom off at his apartment. The Southern Cross Mercantile left Tom with an uneasy feeling as he approached the front door. The sensation was not easily identified but the old familiar building seemed somehow less substantial, almost as if it were in danger of slipping into the mists of Avalon. Tom shook off the unsettling impression and bounded up the stairs to what now seemed an extremely prosaic apartment. After a quick shower and donning of more appropriate attire, he was back on the street headed for the *First Watch*.

"They've finally tipped their hand, ole boy, and it ain't a pretty sight," Preston, now back in his office, was clearly relieved to see his coconspirator in the long struggle to protect their precious Harbor District from the clutches of the land developers and the wrecking ball. "Mildred Masude, on the metro government desk, was at the planning commission meeting when your ex father-in-law and his cronies slipped an unscheduled item on the agenda. Tom, they've lined up the mayor and city council behind a condemnation ordinance to gut the district to make way for a 'renewal' project that will take everything on Front Street from this building all the way down two blocks past your apartment building. Our little strategy has just been trumped."

Their strategy, which had for several years seemed to be working, involved using Preston's wallet and line-of-credit to purchase options on strategically selected pieces of district property in an effort to block attempts to acquire enough land to put together any development that would threaten the integrity and character of the ethnically rich and historically significant community. The flaw in the plan had been their failure to consider the ability of wealth to seduce politicians into corrupt abuses of government power. *Immanent domain* was a "right" of government that had trampled the rights of citizens for time out of mind and it increasingly seemed to carry the force of *manifest destiny* in state courts.

"They are proposing a government/ private sector collaboration to be known as the Greater Metropolitan Waterfront Partnership. The GMWP board will parcel out elements of the development plan to the 'best' bidders to create a new commercial/recreational harbor complex similar to Baltimore's. There's a lot of juice behind this one because they've already received millions in grants from various federal agencies as well as millions more in government backed low interest loans. It would take all the lawyers in Philadelphia and the combined resources of the FBI and CIA to unravel all the pockets that are going to get lined through this scheme. My sources tell me that the *Examiner* will break the story tomorrow and that Chip Worthington has been promised a seat on the GMWP board. I've lost the money I've invested in options because you know they're going to "steal" all the land covered by the condemnation. We're even going to lose the paper since by the time we could relocate there would be nothing left worth printing. I'm afraid the smart money would be on our being screwed, Partner."

Tom had listened without saying a word or even showing much emotion. "What would Blackbeard do?" he muttered under his breath.

"Did I hear you right? Are you OK, Tom?" Preston's concern was sincere. They both had put a huge chunk of their lives into what now seemed a crumbling dream.

"Yeah, I'm fine. I was just wondering what it would take to put a major monkey wrench in their machinery. Call me naive but I still subscribe to the notion that the pen is mightier than swords and greedy politicians."

"I like your attitude, champ, but even if you wrote the ultimate manifesto, we don't have enough circulation to make a dent in public opinion. And you're sure as hell not going to get anything in the *Examiner*."

They sat in silence, as thoughts swirled so furiously that it was a wonder the window blinds didn't rattle. Finally, Preston laughed out loud and exclaimed, "I feel like George Peppard cause 'I love it when a plan comes together.' Tom, I've always known you were too talented to be writing columns for me and we're way past worrying about the success of *First Watch*. We're going to do David one better and kill two birds with one stone. I'm going to pay you to write a novel that will dramatize the virtues of this community while exposing the villainy of these damn carpetbaggers!"

Tom had to laugh as well, "Preston, I'm not at all sure that two birds are 'better' than one Goliath, but I could never pass up an opportunity to relieve you of some of your ill gotten gain. If I write like hell and you simultaneously try to find us a publisher who will fast track the book, we just might derail this run-away train!"

"In the meantime I'll get legal working on every delaying tactic in their bag of tricks to give you as much time as possible. There's nothing to be gained by your writing the great American novel if it hits the bookstores too late to stop this thing. I know your skill and your feel for the subject, Tom. The question is 'Do you have enough fire in your belly to really go after this thing?' Because unless you take the gloves off and fight for keeps, these guys will PR your novel below the fold or, worse yet, turn it back on you and make you the heavy."

Tom considered what Preston had said. He saw in his mind's eye the precious inhabitants of the district, the shops, the restaurants, the market. He thought about a wrecking ball laying waste to over two hundred years of architecture and history. He heard the "old man's" condescension and felt the bite of the words "little writer man."

Hell yes, he had enough fire in his belly. He would rather go down with guns blazing than walk away from this fight. This was war, his war.

Chapter Ten

Fire in the Belly

For the next several weeks Tom worked like a man possessed. Relieved of his duties at *First Watch*, he turned all of his attention and energy toward the novel. Time became meaningless as the writing continued all hours of the day and night. Only Cooper's ministrations saved him from starvation and dehydration.

At first he worked at his apartment but it became unbearably lonely during those hours between his "feedings". Then too, the atmosphere was changing outside on the streets. Through the great arched window he could see the surveyors with their transits shooting the footprints of future buildings and marking their calls on the sidewalks and streets in garish colors of spray paint. Everywhere there was nervousness in people's voices and fear written behind their eyes. It was too much. Tom retreated first to Cooper's apartment further uptown, then finally to the tranquility of the cove.

There, working and living aboard *Cathlene's Dream*, the rhythms of nature began to moderate Tom's frantic activity and offer some much needed perspective. Soon he was falling into a much more nurturing schedule of rising with the sun and, even though he still wrote long after sunset, at least he paused in reflection each evening to witness that glorious last light of the day. He even took small breaks from his laptop to assist Campy with his simple chores. Under the influence of this simplicity, Tom's heart began to soften. He started to long for the peace he had briefly experienced in dialogue with cyber lady. What had she said about wants and needs? Did that have any bearing on the struggle in the district? These and other questions had set up housekeeping in Tom's consciousness.

Then one afternoon while Tom and Campy were cleaning some bait tanks, Pete walked by with a shoulder load of lumber for rebuilding the ramp at the last dock, "Tom, you're startin' to look a little peaked eatin' your own vittles. Why don't you come up and chow down with Campy and me at suppertime."

The sea bass, slaw, and hush puppies were still warming Tom's innards when the three men settled down on the side porch. For a long time the silence was broken only by an occasional belch or some other male sign of satisfaction or passing gastronomical distress. Finally Pete mused aloud, "Reckon that book must be awful important to take up so much of your time."

Tom gave the implied question the time for consideration that it deserved and then, "I thought so when I started, Pete. I had a lot of anger in my gut over the prospect of those bastards and their money coming in and destroying a lot of lives and priceless property."

"Hard to do anything well with anger in your heart. When Cathlene got took I reckon I was so angry with the Almighty that I couldn't do anything for quite a spell. Then, in time, I figured there were still things that mattered to me that needed my tendin'. Guess you could say I came to realize that we're all a-comin' and a-goin' pretty much all the time and we don't have much of a hold on anything except our caring for things. Those men you are holding such hard feelings for aren't planning to do anything that a direct hit by some strong storm wouldn't do. Maybe less. Would you be as angry over that?"

"I don't know, Pete. How would you handle seeing the marina being blown out to sea?"

"It'd hurt alright. And it could happen anytime. How angry I was might tell how much I have learned by what I've lost already. I don't know, Son, these are things that are beyond me. Don't know why I'm even yappin'."

Campy shifted uneasily in his chair, "This makes me sad, Pete. Don't want to have nothin' hurtin' you or Miss Emily. I like Tom too. I'm gonna get Caroline her supper now."

As the old fellow made his way down the hill, Tom and Pete said nothing more. Sometimes the most important task at hand is feeding the cat.

The next day Tom drove into the city and parked behind the Southern Cross Mercantile. For some reason, he chose to wait to go in until after he finished his business. As he walked along Front Street toward the *First Watch* office, he had a hard knot in his stomach. Gus's was closed. The Chinn's Sea Chest Cleaners was being raised. The door to Mexico Lindo was open but the restaurant was empty and Mimmo was nowhere in sight. Everywhere there was construction dust and noise.

Tom opened the front door of *First Watch* and listened for any sound of occupancy. "Is anybody there?" he shouted. No answer. He ran up the stairs and opened Preston's office door.

Preston was in the act of packing his briefcase, "We've lost, partner. It's all going up in smoke. There's no need for legal ploys or public relations. Hell, everybody panicked and started to sell at once. Everything is gone and there wasn't a shot fired. I'm leaving for the Keys but I'll continue to send your checks until the novel is finished. Still, I'm afraid you'll be on your own in getting it published."

"No, Preston, that's why I'm here. I'm returning what you've paid me so far. I don't have the stomach for writing the novel I started and that you've been paying for. I'm so sorry about the paper and everything. God, most of all I'm sorry for all the money you've lost over this thing. We've screwed the pooch on this one."

"Well, the amusing thing is, ole boy, I'm going to end up making a small fortune off this misadventure. And I insist that you, at least, keep the money I've paid you already."

Tom felt confused, "I don't understand. What about all those options that now aren't worth the paper they're written on? And what about your investment in *First Watch*?"

"Seems as if I'm a classic example of the guy who's lucky instead of smart. Those A-holes who work for your ex father-in-law decided to kick us while we were down and removed the paper's property from the condemnation development plan to keep me from recouping any of my investment through the city's land acquisition program. Turned out though that First Land Resorts, Ltd. wanted to build a high-rise condo complex on the edge of the city's project without having to line the pockets of the developers. *Voila*, guess whose property was perfectly positioned? And, as if that weren't enough, the feds are forcing the developers to expand the development to include empowerment zones and that means buying a ton of my optioned land without the benefit of the condemnation. What's more, federal guidelines determine the procedure for appraising the property values so you might say I'm making out like a bandit in spite of myself and my enemies. Bottom line, I'm going to be even more stinking rich than I was when I bought the paper and took up the cause."

"I'm really glad for you, Preston. It's good that something positive can come from this mess. I'll miss seeing your ugly, rich face though. When did you let everyone go? I haven't talked with Cooper all week and I didn't hear about the closing."

"Actually, the paper closed a month ago. I think Cooper hasn't told you because she didn't want to disturb your writing. That's a damn fine lady, Tom. I hope you realize she is head over heels in love with you. If you ask me, you're the wealthy one here."

"I think I've been afraid to look at that square in the eyes. There's no doubt that she is the best friend I've ever had and has probably been the best thing that has ever happened to me. But love, damn, Preston, I'm not sure I could ever be the person she deserves in a mate."

"All I can say is if you screw this one up and let her get away, God isn't likely to look kindly on that kind of stupidity. Wake up, knucklehead, you are blessed. You have been given everything on a silver platter. Enjoy what you've been given."

The words had a familiar ring. Did truth always feel like *de ja vu*? Tom realized that some things couldn't be put off forever.

Chapter Eleven

A-comin' and A-goin'

The condemned sign and chained front door at the Southern Cross Mercantile seemed to fit the circumstances to a tee. This was the exclamation point at the end of a chapter that must have been destined to end in just this way at just this time.

Without even giving a thought to the belongings he had left in his apartment, Tom walked around to the back of the building and started his car. A few blocks later it dawned on him that he was headed for Cooper's apartment.

"I can see in your eyes that you have been to the district. I'm so sorry, Tommy. I haven't known how to tell you. It all happened so fast and with such finality. Here, come sit down and rest. I know this is too much to take in."

Her expression spoke of such compassion and tenderness that Tom had to choke back a tear. "No, I'm the one that's sorry, Coup. I should have been here with you. I should have done something. Helped Preston, said 'goodbye' to some of our friends, shot somebody, Hell, I don't know what, but at the very least, I should have been with you."

"Tommy, believe me; there was nothing for you or anyone else to do. When I heard that the Southern Cross was coming down, I brought your things over to my spare bedroom and gave them Pete's address for sending your rent refund check. The only encouragement that any of us could find in all of this was that you finally had an opportunity to do some serious writing and no one wanted to see that interrupted."

Tom shifted uneasily on the couch and his action was immediately met with a look of understanding and resolve from Cooper, "This is no good. Neither one of us can sit here in this apartment at a time like this. Let's roll down all the windows in the woodie and drive down to the cove. We'll head out to sea and sail all night if we feel like it."

Cooper had been right: moving, whether in the woodie or on *Cathlene's Dream*, had brought relief even if it had been an exercise in the illusion of escape. In truth, they escaped from nothing. Everything that had happened rode with them like an extra passenger but somehow it all seemed more bearable in the context of greater space and wind blowing in their faces.

On the second day they realized in unison that it was time to return to the "world."

Tom had made it clear that he didn't want to talk or think about the abortive novel or anything else for that matter. He just wanted to help Pete and Campy around the marina and, hopefully, reconnect with his equilibrium. For Cooper the break from work in the city was a blessing. She would live with Pete so Tom could continue on board the boat. Maybe it was time for her to move back to the cove for good. Time would tell.

And, as surely as the sun comes up and the moon whispers secrets to the dark water, things did start to fall back into an easy pattern of simple chores, soft laughter, and familiar faces. In fact, Tom began to recognize more and more of the faces that belonged to the boats that he had almost forgotten to think of as having "owners."

Everyone was on a first name basis regardless of his or her age or standing in the cove's pecking order, if indeed there was such a thing. There was a paradoxical blend of openness and sensitivity to privacy among the cove's inhabitants that was far too complex to ever be reduced to a code of etiquette. One just had to feel one's way along and remain conscious of the nuances of facial expression, tone of voice, and body language to sense where the boundaries were and then scrupulously observe them.

Since Tom had stopped writing, he had much more time on his hands than his apprentice duties with Pete and Campy required. And so he looked around for a more formidable windmill at which to tilt. It was then that he realized that Campy's houseboat, although extremely well built, was in much need of repair. And after carefully broaching the subject with the old gentleman, a full blown remodeling project was planned and put into motion.

Campy seemed to be genuinely pleased by all the attention and he was consulted on every detail of design, material, and finish. Still, his enthusiasm and appreciation could not be matched with energy and effort. Most afternoons Campy just sat in his rocking chair on the front porch of the boat with Caroline sleeping cozily in his lap. His days of chores had come to an end and it was time for him to enjoy a well-deserved rest from his labors. Tom came and went with materials and tools and enjoyed the special peace that he derived from working around the dozing friends.

Toward the end of the remodeling, Tom arrived one morning with touch-up paint and stain and was greeted by a handsome middle-aged man with a very slender frame and gray around the temples of his neatly trimmed hair.

"Hi, I'm Paul, an old friend of Campy's. Campy has been telling me all about the improvements you have made to the boat. Caroline seems pretty excited too."

"Pleased to meet you, Paul. I think I've seen you around here before. Do you keep a boat here?"

"Yeah, I inherited the *Unattached* from my parents. They were among the first to throw in with Pete and we've been here pretty much ever since. I don't get out here from the city as often as I would like but every time I return it's like I never left."

Tom liked Paul at once and recognized some quality he could not put his finger on but that felt more like meeting an old friend than a stranger.

"I think I know just what you mean. I remember a poem I read once that had a line 'some part of us had always been there, some part would always remain' and I've had just that impression ever since I arrived at the cove."

"Sounds to me like you're a goner, friend. Better start looking for a boat. We don't take to landlubbers around here, you know," laughed Paul.

Campy roused from his reverie. Of late he had fallen into long lapses of silence that seemed more like daydreaming than sleep, "Tom will make a good sailor, Paul. Tom likes to work and he likes Miss Emily. Tom is home here."

"Well, that's all the endorsement I need. Tom, you still need a boat, you know. We'll not have you skulking around lusting after other folk's vessels. You start saving your pennies and working on your seamanship. I'll bet a boat will show up with your name on it before you know it."

Sadly that was the only time the three were together. The following Sunday, Tom stopped by Campy's to check on his friend. Campy was in the rocking chair with Caroline in his lap as usual. Only this time, Campy's nap was eternal. Tom's tears flowed without restraint and all he could do was sit and feel the sacred silence.

When Tom arrived at Pete's, Cooper opened the door, looked into his eyes and put her arms around him and sobbed. "I knew it was coming but there was no way to prepare. O God, this is going to hurt Pete so bad."

By the afternoon of Campy's funeral, Tom had learned that Paul was known as Father Paul outside the cove where he served as rector of a large congregation in the city. And, as the inhabitants of the cove gathered at the tiny graveyard on the side of the hill just up from Pete's cottage, it was Paul who stood after a hymn and scripture and faced the stricken gathering.

"We are gathered here today to celebrate the life and mark the passing of our friend, George Finley Macgregor, known to us all as 'Campy'.

"When Campy was born some 81 years ago just outside Edinburgh, one can only imagine that his parents aspired to a very different life for their infant son. Perhaps they wished to see him become a scholar, a barrister, or a physician destined to heal and save lives. Don't we all hold such dreams of success for our children?

"As I prepared these remarks for this special occasion, I thought about how different the aspirations must be as our heavenly Father welcomes each of His children into this world. As He unfolds each tiny, tender heart and sets it free to discover the world and itself, what must be His wish for its destiny?

"Someone once wrote that there is no wisdom greater than kindness. If so, is there one among us wiser than Campy?

"Faith, hope, and love endureth, but the greatest of these is love. Have we known a purer love than Campy's?

"Our Master said that we must become as little children in order to enter heaven. Can anyone imagine heaven without Campy?

"No, as parents, we might consider reexamining our aspirations for our children...and ourselves, and try remembering where we are going and what our journey is all about. Perhaps then we, like Campy, may end our days on earth with the ultimate affirmation of 'Well done, thou good and faithful servant.'

"Miss Emily has been known to observe that no one ever really leaves this Cove. Surely we make a heart investment in the souls gathered here and in this beautiful natural expression of God's handiwork. And, perhaps, just as surely we leave an indelible impression on those who share our love and passion for this place. I know I will never cease to walk this ground or sail this water without feeling some lasting sense of those who have shared this place, this life, with me. Campy, I will treasure your company in spirit as deeply as I have valued your friendship in life."

Chapter Twelve

Company in Spirit

The simple little man left an enormous hole in the community. Yet everyone was most concerned about the hole in Pete's heart. Cooper and Tom stayed close to the cottage, as Pete seemed unable to summon the will to resume his duties around the marina.

After a few days Tom started looking after things around the docks and Cooper continued to spend her days and nights with her dad. She used the excuse that she was behind on the marina's bookkeeping that she had taken over in her teens. Pete just sat in his favorite chair on the side porch looking out across the water.

In truth, Tom was relieved to have something physical to occupy his body and vacate his wounded mind and spirit. It took some will power, however, to return to the tasks he had shared with Campy. At first he felt even more empty moving about the docks heavy with the absence of his friend and workmate. Then little by little he started to understand what Paul had said about treasuring Campy's company in spirit. In doing even the simplest chores that they had once shared, Tom found himself smiling over small flashes of memory. At other times in quiet moments of rest or reflection, he could "feel" his old friend's spirit. Then he began to "talk" to this familiar presence and realized that a new dimension had been added to his life, one that left him more whole and grounded.

Tom was just finishing his afternoon chores when he noticed Oliver Newton quietly engaged in maintenance aboard his boat, the *Star Waltz*. Following a deep-seated intuition, Tom walked along side the antique boat's slip and addressed the old sailor.

"Oliver, I don't wish to intrude but I have been admiring *Star Waltz* since I first visited the cove. Would it be a good time for me to take a closer look?"

Oliver studied Tom for a moment and then without changing expression or interrupting his chores, "Come aboard, Lad. I welcome your company. Feel free to move about topside and below while I finish up here."

No Virgo female could have maintained so spotless a vessel. Every surface, whether bulkhead or deck, was immaculately polished and every item of gear was stowed in its proper locker perfectly coiled, folded, or wrapped. There was nothing extraneous. Everything had an essential, even vital, purpose in the smooth operation of the boat. Tom was struck by the idea that for Oliver sailing was not a diversion or a means to an end. Sailing was the end.

On returning to the weather deck, Tom found Oliver sitting in the cockpit as though waiting for Tom and inviting conversation.

"I notice a complete lack of electric navigational equipment on board, not even a radio or GPS. Am I missing something?"

Oliver smiled, "You really are a writer. That is not only a keen observation but you have immediately grasped the heart of the matter.

"Don't let gadgets come between you and the experience of sailing. Being in a boat with the proper attitude is as close as we mortals will ever get to being caught up in the majesty and mystery of creation. Everything you are capable of sensing at sea is important to an awareness of your role in the universe. More than just winds and currents, stars and clouds, every subtle shade and texture of the water, every sound and scent, even the birds and fish, have important information to share with those who will observe over time and seek to learn.

"You see, there are no shortcuts. Too many people rush through life trying to reach the next destination without realizing that the journey is our gift. Gadgets are used as a shortcut to learning as if learning were an obstacle to our moving ahead. To my mind, on the other hand, learning is more important than any destination or acquisition. Learning is the very means by which we communicate with our Maker.

"A good sail is like a prayer. It is an opportunity to listen to creation speaking to us in so many different ways that we become lost in, or perhaps assume our rightful place in, all that God has made. And like all prayer, we don't change God; we just learn more about how to move around in his handiwork with greater skill and gratitude.

"Don't get me wrong, Tom. I'm not trying to tell you how it is. 'How it is' is mostly mystery. I wouldn't have it any other way; otherwise, somebody would be trying to copy write it and sell it on TV or use it to appear better than the rest of us. All I'm really doing is telling you why I sail and why I don't take with gadgets on board my boat."

Tom smiled at this. He realized that he really liked, even respected, Oliver. After a moment of reflection, Tom surprised himself at his own boldness when he asked, "Oliver, I think I want to be like you when I grow up and I would really like to sail with you and gain your knowledge of the sea and sailing. Think that would be possible?"

Oliver looked Tom straight in the eye and simply said "Nope."

Tom was just recovering from the embarrassment of the rebuff when the old sailor continued, "Don't get me wrong, Lad. I believe I would enjoy having you aboard for some sailing but you won't be acquiring my knowledge. Let me see if I can explain.

"First, knowledge that is spoon fed is materially different from knowledge that is borne of personal observation and experience, knowledge that you had to dig for yourself, so to speak.

"Second, knowledge is a very personal commodity. No two people have the same knowledge. Knowledge, unlike information, cannot be stored outside the human heart and mind. Information can be written down or stored in a computer as electronic data, but access to this information does not automatically foster understanding or even the ability to profit from its use.

"Knowledge is comprised of two basic parts. On the one hand, you have the more or less objective reality of that which is being observed and, on the other, you have all of the filters of prior experience and personal bias of the observer through which the raw data of the objective reality must pass in order to be perceived by the observer. This duality of observation makes all knowledge unique to the individual who carries it in his memory.

"There is no way to escape this bias. Even when a given so-called objective object or event is captured as data by an inanimate recorder, the experience and bias of the person who designed the recording instrument as well as the protocol for selecting its location and the timing of its operation profoundly influence the nature of the data collected. Choices as simple as whether to record visual light or sound or other forms of energy, or whether to sample a very large field of 'observation' or focus on a minute target will obviously yield very different results even if the data is never interpreted. Then imagine how much more personal the observation if the data ***is*** viewed and evaluated by a human following its collection.

"No, I'm afraid the most I can do is make some suggestions as to how you might want to go about building your own knowledge of the sea. In the long run, it will be of much greater value to you. It will then carry with it the richness of your own experiences and will feed your heart and soul even as it serves your will in assisting with your passage through this life whether on land or the majestic deep."

Tom was dumbfounded, “My god, Oliver, you are a poet and a philosopher.”

The old man smiled, “I’ve never known a good sailor who wasn’t a philosopher at heart and, for me at least, sailing is poetry. But philosophy can be dangerous. If you put too fine an edge on the philosophical sword you wield, you can end up shedding your own blood. You see, the philosophy of sailors derives from their own experience.

“The sterile philosophy of scholars that comes from reading books is lacking in the moral compass that only heart-directed experience can provide. Thus, we are really back to the difference between information and knowledge.”

That, as it turned out, was only the first of many tutorials that Oliver conducted over the following months, as Tom became a frequent mate aboard the *Star Waltz*. And just as there is no stronger bond than a shared passion, the ancient mariner and his protégé became the best of friends, the kind of significant presences in ones life that help define its meaning.

Chapter Thirteen

Family

We are given a family of blood in much the same manner that we inherit our physical characteristics and talents. These givens may seem like gifts or they may be experienced as curses or straightjackets from which we cannot escape. Then there is the family that spirit and we conspire to assemble as we make our way along our long succession of choices that we call life. Even with this accumulated informal family of friends, can we ever be sure how much we really had to do with their selection?

In much the same way, a man of the cloth is assigned his flock, warts and all, and surely must question in his heart the wisdom of some of his assignments. As with the affinities of secular families, however, most ministers seem to collect an informal band of souls whose needs seem to be his to shepherd without assignment from his "superiors."

So it was with Father Paul and the inhabitants of the cove. And it was this informal spiritual calling which led him to take a few days away from his congregation in the city and drive down to the marina to look in on his friend Pete and attend to the bruised hearts and spirits of Campy's little chosen family.

What was it about the cove? This question played in the back of Paul's mind as he headed down the coast highway. Why did a visit to the marina always carry with it a renewal of spirit that left him wondering whether he was on a mission of service or on a pilgrimage for the benefit of his own soul? Or, just maybe, there was no difference between the two, merely two faces of the same reality.

Tom saw Paul seated with Pete on the side porch of the cottage and instinctively knew to pass quietly to the front door. Cooper met him as he entered the kitchen, “Paul showed up this morning and has been with Pete for almost two hours now. Can I get you some coffee? It’s fresh.”

“Sure, thanks.” Tom looked through the screen door toward the two men sitting quietly side-by-side, “wonder if Paul knew how low Pete has been? What am I saying; of course, he had to know. Wonder if he can snap Pete out of it?”

“I doubt if he is trying. I suspect he is just being a friend and showing his support and caring. The healing Pete needs is within him and he will recover when he has been able to get his heart around his loss." Cooper's observation was not spoken as a correction or even as instruction, just sharing and in much the same tone as she might speak to herself. "By the way, Paul said that he needs to speak with you and me together while he is here. Shall I invite him back up for dinner tonight?"

That evening Pete was quiet during dinner and excused himself and headed for his bedroom just as Cooper was bringing in coffee and desert. Even so, Pete's affection for his clerical friend was obvious and equally clear was his appreciation for Paul's presence.

"There's too much magic in the air this evening to be shut up inside. Let's have our desert and coffee on the porch," Cooper offered as a not too subtle attempt to lighten the mood by changing the venue.

True enough, the air was delicious and the color of the last rays of sunset seemed to mark the end of something and suggest the beginning of a new and more mysterious chapter filled with promise and challenge. After giving Cooper's homemade key lime pie the reverence it so richly deserved, Paul put down his fork and cleared his throat as one who was about to embark upon a subject that required focus and deliberation.

"My friend Campy had an exaggerated opinion of my role in this world and often invested me with duties that were, at the very least, peculiar to my calling. He was very aware that his time with us was drawing to a close and he could feel his flame beginning to dim. On my last visit with him, he asked me to draw up a will for him to sign. I'm not at all sure that it is a legally binding document and I am quiet sure that I broke a least one law by 'practicing law' without a license. Nevertheless, since his meager possessions were largely of sentimental value, I believe that the net effect of my action was to obligate myself to the rather daunting task of tracking down his beneficiaries and conveying their inheritances. Which brings me to the two of you.

"The one thing Campy owned that had monetary value was his houseboat and he left it to his two good friends, Miss Emily and Tom.

Paul paused for a moment because by this time both Tom and Cooper were softly crying. They took each other's hand and Cooper leaned her head on Tom's shoulder.

As the tide of emotion began to subside, Paul continued, "I did check with Pete because I realized there was some question as to the actual ownership of the boat, but Pete said that as surely as anyone ever owned anything that boat belonged to Campy. He had earned every board and nail that had gone into it.

"I'm not certain as to what documentation is appropriate in a situation like this and I'll leave that to the two of you to sort out. Campy did make a request that you care for Caroline. I suspect that he realized that she would be most comfortable with you and he probably also knew that she would not be coaxed away from the boat. Pete told me that you have been going down there every day to feed her and that no one has seen her off the boat's porch since Campy died. If humans were given to that kind of loyalty there would likely be a good bit less misery in this world, don't you think?

"There is one more thing. This is, uh, rather delicate. Please forgive me if I appear to be intruding on your private lives; I guess I am but I assure you it is out of loving concern and not out of judgment.

"You see, when I asked Pete about the matter of the houseboat's ownership, he also expressed a genuine concern about the nature of your relationship. His love for Cooper is, of course, unquestionable and, you may be assured, there is no one on this planet he would rather have as a son-in-law than you, Tom. I do believe, however, he is extremely worried about Tom's commitment to you, Cooper, and is frightened that you will be seriously hurt if your current relationship should not end in marriage."

An electrical storm in the cove itself would have been no match for the fire that flared in Cooper's eyes as she bounded from her chair. For a split second Paul must have feared being hit on the nose and, truth is, Cooper may have been closer to clobbering her old friend than either of them would, to this day, like to admit.

"Damn it to hell and back again! If that doesn't freeze hell over I don't know what will! Let's just get one damn thing straight right this minute! I love Tommy more than I ever thought possible and I damn well know that he feels the same way about me. We don't need no stinking priest to bless what we have found in each other and I sure as hell don't need Pete, no matter how much he's hurting, sticking his damn nose in my business! I can just see me screwing up our relationship by pushing Tommy into something he isn't ready for yet—something he may never be ready for. And I can just hear my goddamn vows, 'I Emily Cathlene Cooper do hog tie you Tommy Foster into this damn union because I don't have enough faith in you to give you my heart without involving every damn institution of church and state to do what our love can't.' Goddamn you, Paul. You, of all people, should know better!"

With a beet-red face wet with tears, Cooper stormed into the house slamming the screen door half off its hinges. The two men had shrunk into their chairs and just sat in the ringing silence.

Finally Paul spoke in a soft, measured voice, "I thought that went well, didn't you?"

Chapter Fourteen

Guidance

When it was clear that Cooper wasn't going to make another appearance that evening, if ever, Tom and Paul wandered down the hill to the docks. The discovery of an unopened bottle of single malt, twelve-year-old scotch on board *Cathlene's Dream* was sufficient excuse for a marathon examination of the universe and the underlying causes of the world's problems.

An hour or so later when the alcohol had loosened the last vestiges of inhibition, Tom got around to what had been occupying most of his waking thoughts and a fair share of his dream time as well, "Paul, old buddy, this is going to come as a very big shock to you but the shameful fact is I'm pretty much fucked up. How in the hell can any man in possession of his faculties fail to rush into a committed relationship with someone like Cooper just because he is haunted by the faceless image of some phantom of cyberspace?"

"Yes, Cooper has told me about your experiences with this mysterious chat-room person. She said that you know almost nothing about this person. As I understand, you don't even know whether you were sharing with a male or female, not that it makes a lot of difference, I guess."

"You just hit the nail square on the head, Old Chum. What does make any difference? If, before I met Cooper, I had made a list of all the 'things' that were important to me in a woman,

I don't think the resultant composite would have resembled Cooper in the least. So, obviously, those traits don't mean squat because I love Cooper more than I would ever have thought possible for me to love anyone. So why the hell can't I get past this obsession with a person that has no discernible traits at all? I feel like a dog chasing its tail. I not only don't know anything about anything but I don't have a clue as to where to start looking for some freaking answers. Got any wisdom you'd like to contribute?"

Paul couldn't help smiling at his befuddled friend, "Well, I'm reasonably sure that wisdom, like beauty, is pretty much in the eye of the beholder. And I'm equally convinced that you have access to all the answers that appear to be eluding you. You see, if we don't have the ability to not only access truth but also to recognize or validate that truth when we find it, then we're lost without a compass to guide our way. Who would we believe if not ourselves? And how would we ever know that we were listening to the right guru if we didn't have that ability to recognize and validate?"

"Damn, Paul, you sound just like cyber lady. Sure you're not the one who's fucking up my life? I have a few dates for which you had better have air tight alibis."

"Sorry, Charlie, but it isn't going to be that easy. My guess is that you can't 'get past' this other identity because you have a deep-seated need to know what that person is trying to say to you and to understand what that person represents for you. My experience has led me to believe that anything or anyone that has such a profound impact on our lives carries great meaning for us and represents some aspect of who we are or what we need to be doing in order to fulfill our life's purpose."

"Well, assuming for a moment that is so, why all the damn secrecy and why all the infernal riddles? Why not just spit it out and say 'I'm Madam Rose from Hoboken and I'm here to lay some really heavy shit on you so you can clean up your act and move on to discover penicillin'?"

"Only guessing, of course, but what if the process of discovering these things is as important as the answers themselves?"

"Now that really sounds familiar. My seagoing philosopher, Oliver Newton, said something very similar to me not long ago."

"Oliver is one interesting fellow. I don't think I've ever had a conversation with him in which I didn't learn something. Pete told me you have been sailing with him quite a bit lately. That's something. I've never known him to take anyone with him before except for Cooper when she was in her teens."

"Cooper deserves a lot better than me, Paul. How can I ever deserve to be with her with this damn distraction hanging over me?"

"That's one you're going to have to answer for yourself. But just for the sake of argument, have you ever considered the possibility that you are cyber lady?"

"What the hell are you saying? Are you suggesting that I am lying or that I am nuts?"

"There's always the chance that both are true, you know. But, no, what occurs to me to wonder is whether there is any reason to consider that your subconscious, or maybe even your higher self, has been sending you these digital messages to guide you out of a very dark period of your life. After all, think about how much your life has changed for the better since you 'discovered' this person on your computer. If I understand what Cooper has told me, it sure seems to me that almost every aspect of your life began to move in a new direction as a result of that first cyber chat. And wouldn't that explain the secrecy? Would you have paid the same attention to a message you knew you had written to yourself?"

"At least one of us has had too much to drink. It's going to be really interesting to wake up tomorrow and see what this sounds like cold sober. Then there's always the possibility that I won't remember any of this or, worse, that I will remember and then find out that you drove back to the city right after Cooper went to bed."

"I believe you're getting the hang of this, Tom."

Chapter Fifteen

Lulu

Just as God gives us bright, unused new days, so we are empowered, should we choose, to give ourselves and each other fresh starts free of guilt and recrimination. It was just such a day and opportunity when Tom awoke with a waterlogged loaf of bread where his brain was supposed to be. Unfortunately he did remember the night before and he certainly had any number of physical reminders of that bottle of scotch.

After an unsteady ascent of the hill, Tom entered the cottage to find Cooper with her arms around Paul's neck.

"You're just lucky I didn't have a weapon at my disposal," she laughed. "Today I remember that I love you, though, for the life of me, I can't remember why!"

"Well, I was once again reminded of the O'Malley female pirates and thought myself fortunate that those genes have had a few generations to be diluted. Cooper, I am sorry I got your Irish up. I was way out of line, Lass."

Tom cleared his throat, "First you get me drunk and now I find you in the arms of my gal. What kind of priest are you?"

"Don't worry, Tommy, he's lousy in the sack. Hasn't had a date in years and probably hasn't seen a naked girl since we were preteens trying to figure things out."

"Never could abide a girl who kisses and tells," frowned Paul. "And, speaking of wayward women, are you any closer to the identity of that cyber chick who stole your heart, Tom?"

"You best let that one go, Super Cleric! Did you know that this Bozo actually had the balls to suggest that I was writing those notes to myself?" It was not clear whether Tom was joking, not even to himself.

"Boys, you just simmer down and play nice or you won't be getting any of the pancakes I have mixed up over there. Besides, the thought had crossed my mind too, Tommy. She only shows up when you're by yourself and, truth be told, she does sound a lot like you think."

"Yeah, Tom, and, anyway, what difference does it really make? Whether it's you, your higher self, a bored priest with too much time on his hands, an angel, an alien, or the Almighty, since this entity obviously has no intention of ever revealing his or herself in the flesh, where can this thing go beyond giving you an opportunity to look more closely at your life?"

Tom had regained control and paused before responding in an exaggerated calm and deliberate manner, "Don't you think that has occurred to me? Don't you see that I'm not obsessing over this phantom like a love-struck schoolboy? My quest was from the start an attempt to recover a sense of well being that came from my encounters with this 'person.' By now, I'm not even sure I remember what that feeling was like and I'm quite certain that I don't need that 'fix' the way I did when it first occurred. I am equally certain that this is a topic that has worn me and itself out and needs to be consigned to the dustbin of eternity."

Paul grinned, "No, this is way too much fun to just drop, especially when it's at lover boy's expense. As I believe I noted last night, your life, Tom, really has improved since your first encounter with cyber lady and by now you probably don't need that 'rush' as much as you did earlier. The one thought I would leave you with as I escape to my relatively mundane life in the city, is that the 'high' you experienced can't be sustained by anyone no matter who they are with or what they are doing. If there had been a 'body' attached to those messages and its inhabitant had been willing to meet you or even to live with you for the rest of your life, you still would have lost the 'feeling' in time.

"As I suggested before, the strong 'hit' you felt was probably a sign that there was something of great importance attached to your encountering either the message or the messenger, or both. If it was the message then it's important to remember that there is no energy, euphoric or otherwise, attached to information. Only when information is processed by the heart does it become wisdom. And only when wisdom is lived can it begin to transform us cell by cell until it is truly 'written in our hearts' and then has the effect of changing our energy and the quality of our being. Mystics don't engage in spiritual disciplines to be pious; they understand that only through mindful application of wisdom to their daily lives can they move from knowledge to enlightenment.

"If, on the other hand, this is all about the messenger, then you are still stuck with the task of determining the identity of cyber lady or, at least, discovering what meaning he/she has for your life. If it's both, then you need to give me a call in a few decades and let me know how things are progressing."

"Would you two morons just stop," Cooper feigned exasperation and shook her fist at both of her loves. "I'm going to start these flapjacks and if I hear another word about spiritual anything I'm going to take this skillet and brain both of you!"

Not ready to risk a repeat of last night's blow up, Paul threw up his hands in a gesture of surrender, "I give up. Change of subject. I do have one more task before I leave. After breakfast I think it will be time for me to introduce Tom to my friend, Lulu."

Tom caught the twinkle in both of their eyes and the slight hint of conspiratorial mirth as their eyes briefly met and quickly averted, "I don't know what the two of you have up your sleeves, but I do know that woman has intimidated the hell out of me since the first time I saw her. I don't think I have ever seen anyone with as much presence. You'd think she was an African queen or at least a Supreme Court justice."

"I told you he was a pussy. Want me to come along and hold your hand, baby?"

Tom started to laugh in spite of himself, "Coup, it's at times like this that I know I love you, otherwise I would be forced to rearrange your pretty face."

Following breakfast, Cooper insisted on remaining behind with the dishes while Paul more or less forced Tom down the hill to the docks like a man being led to the gallows. As they approached the *Antigone*, Tom spotted their quarry sitting on a closed hatch reading a book. She was dressed with a casual elegance that defied description and her smooth, flawless black complexion made her age impossible to determine.

"Permission to come aboard with a friend you need to know, Lulu?" Paul's mock formality seemed almost appropriate; given the condescending gaze they received from the luminous yet stern eyes that peered from above the half-lens reading glasses.

"Permission granted. Always a pleasure to see you, Paul, and I'm sure you would not intrude upon my solitude with anyone that was less than enchanting. Actually, I've been wondering how long it would be before Tom ceased regarding me from afar and presented himself for closer inspection. What is the occasion, gentlemen?"

Tom suddenly realized that his instincts had been accurate and that he should have taken heed and stayed as far away from this overpowering monarch as possible. Now it was too late and he felt like a bug under a magnifying glass.

"Well, Lulu it's good to see you too," Paul grinned. "Seems young Foster here has fancied himself an author and has committed many hours to the writing of the great American novel. Then just when we were all ready to help him spend his money and bask in the reflection of his fame, the old boy just quit and left us hanging. Now I don't think we're dealing with ordinary run-of-the-mill writer's block. No, I think the lad has lost his confidence and, what with you being someone who from time to time dabbles in the teaching of writing, I thought you might find it in your legendarily generous heart to tune him back up and turn him loose on an unsuspecting world. What'da ya think?"

"I do not think. I know, that if it were not for the possibility that you possess some special dispensation from the Almighty, I would not tolerate your impudence. Nevertheless, you are here by my leave and I just happen to entertain an interest in Pete's future son-in-law. Would you be so kind as to share your writing with me, Tom?"

Tom was speechless. He had never encountered anyone so presumptuous and, yet, for some reason, he felt almost honored that she had expressed an interest in his work. "Paul didn't forewarn me what he was up to, Lulu...is it ok if I call you that? Furthermore, I'm not sure that anyone is ready to sign me on as Cooper's fiancé. But, in answer to your question, I suppose I would be grateful to have your opinion relative to any potential I might possess as a serious writer. I'm afraid, however, that I have, indeed, lost my appetite for the novel and have no interest in completing it whatever your verdict on its merits."

"As you wish. I do expect you to address me as Lulu. All of my friends do. And, young man, I know what I know whether you have allowed yourself to accept the truth or not. Please bring your novel over at once and then return on Thursday at four o'clock for tea. We shall discuss the wisdom of your career interest at that time."

Having been thus dismissed, there was nothing left to say. Tom headed for *Cathlene's Dream* to fetch the novel while Paul returned to the cottage to say goodbye to Pete and Cooper.

By the time Tom walked into the kitchen, Paul, for his own safety, had already left for the city. "What in the hell did you two think you were doing and who is this woman anyway? One of these days, Coup, ...just one of these days."

As she began to laugh, Tom was reminded of just how damn pretty she was. He could never be angry for long looking into those eyes. In fact, he could look into her face forever without getting tired. He was at total peace looking at her. He was at home.

"She is a very old friend of the family, Tommy. And she not only teaches at the university but she owns a publishing company founded by her grandfather. I understand that she is something of a force in the world of letters."

Tom was thunderstruck, "Lulu. Lucenda. Oh my god, that was Lucenda Westerman! Oh shit! I was giving lip to one of the international giants of literary criticism. Oh shit! I left her my novel. Oh shit!"

By that time, Cooper was splitting her sides with laughter and Tom was hyper-ventilating. For the rest of the evening he never fully recovered his composure. Dinner was unusually warm and pleasant though and Pete seemed to be in somewhat better spirits.

The next two days seemed to drag out endlessly as Tom waited for his tea appointment with Lulu. The one really bright spot was Pete joining Tom for chores. They didn't say a lot but it was apparent that each of them was drawing strength and pleasure from their just being together. Chop wood, carry water. What healing there was in simplicity, especially when enjoyed surrounded by the beauty of the cove.

Finally the appointed hour arrived. After refreshment had been served in the galley, Lulu's face softened and her voice had a sincerity that seemed almost sacred, "Tom, I have been honored to read your work. Your writing is not only tight and wonderfully imaginative, you have a rare ability to capture the divinity of humanity and to inspire your readers to look deeper into their souls and mine the treasure that awaits us all if we know how to look. I understand why you could not find it in your heart to continue your novel with the motivation that had launched your endeavor. Please consider, however, giving life to those wonderful characters with a new perspective. I believe there is an expression, 'don't throw the baby out with the bathwater' that applies here.

Nothing that happened in the harbor district negated the value of the humanity that inspired your passion. Ask yourself what this has meant for those people and how their lives may have changed as a result. I know there is still an important work here and that you have the ability to bring it to fruition. My only advice is that you not force the issue. Like all great writers you are growing with and through your writing. Don't outrun your headlights. Just stay the course and know that I stand ready to assist you when this work is ready to take wings and find its own way in the world."

Tom had left Lulu to find some alone time. Her quiet confidence in him, in his writing, had strangely filled him with humility. True, writing was always a solitary enterprise, yet somehow he knew that it would never again be as lonely, as fragile and dangerous as it had been without her support and appreciation. He remembered what Paul had said about the strong “hit” one felt when meeting someone and how it probably was a sign of something or someone of great importance in one’s life. Now Tom realized that the “hit” was not always experienced as positive in the beginning.

Chapter Sixteen

When Push Comes To Shove

They were almost eight hours out on a four-day sail down the coast when Tom started to feel an intensity of anxiety that was stronger than he had ever experienced and, what was more, there was a surreal almost dream-like quality to everything around him. As the minutes went by the feeling grew stronger to the point that he started to become claustrophobic and just wanted the hell off that boat.

He decided that he needed to say something to Oliver about what was going on and, with that thought, he began to feel some relief. But no sooner than he decided he was just being stupid and didn't need to say anything, the awful anxiety was back full force. He then realized that when he made a move toward Oliver the feeling subsided and the second he would turn in another direction, the anxiety would once again begin to build.

Finally, like a man sleepwalking, Tom moved to Oliver's side at the helm and tried to explain what he was feeling.

It was more a look of concern than a frown that crossed the deep-lined, weathered face of the old sailor. He acknowledged Tom's panic and confusion, "I recognize and respect what you're feeling, Lad. Don't know whether it's something we need to get away from or something we need to get to but it's clear that we need to come about and head back and do it in a hurry. Cell phones and ship-to-shore radios can fail you but, unless you are relying on them too much, what you're experiencing right now can always get through."

For the next two hours they headed back under full sail. Tom scanned the horizon looking for something he couldn't quite name, but still, he just kept expecting something to appear there in the open ocean.

Then it was there. He saw the spray even before he could see the tiny speck that was a boat. He grabbed for Oliver's spyglass and his heart stopped as he made out the shape of the marina's power launch headed straight for them at full throttle.

On the way back to the cove aboard the speeding smaller boat, Tom learned what he seemed to have intuitively already known. There had been an accident, a terrible accident while Cooper had been driving the woodie into the city. Little more was known except that she had been alive but in critical condition when Pete had sent the launch to look for Tom.

Someone must have driven Tom to the hospital and someone must have taken him to the waiting room. So deep was he into his own mind that he seemed to have very little contact with the outside world. Was he communing with himself, with Cooper, with God? Was there a difference?

Then Pete was there. The pain in those gentle eyes was almost too much to bear. “She’s in a bad way, Son. The doctors say the next few hours...” He couldn’t finish as that powerful frame began to quake and he buried his head in his huge hands.

Paul was the next to arrive. His face was pale and there were signs he had been crying; but, as always, he turned his healing attention to others beginning with Pete. A few more friends from the marina began to fill the small dimly-lit, stuffy waiting room but Tom remained in his suspended state, seemingly removed from everything and everyone, until a doctor dressed in green with a surgical mask still hanging around his neck entered the room and was directed over to where Pete was still sitting with Paul. Immediately the three of them left the room leaving behind Tom, now very much alert, and filled with a chilling fear and emptiness more dreadful than anything he had ever felt, even in his most awful ordeals.

After several eternities Paul returned and sat next to Tom, "She may not make it, Tom. The doctors have prepared Pete for making some pretty gruesome decisions and he is sitting with Coup in the ICU. They are only allowing immediate family into the room and this may prove to be more than either Pete or Cooper can take. Cooper has been in a coma since she arrived in the ER and her vital signs are weakening. I know that this is as bad as it gets, my friend, but you and I also know how much she loves you and what a fighter she is. Maybe she will find her 'Irish' and lick this thing."

The hot tears flowing down Tom's cheeks were stinging his skin and he was having trouble swallowing. Through his shallow breathing he managed to thank Paul and then began to rock back and forward in his chair with a violent intensity that only suggested the anger he was directing toward his most vulnerable center. Why had he not been with her, protecting her? What a total pussy he had been for allowing some kind of Goddamn mind games keep him from grabbing her up, marrying her, and spending every moment with her for the rest of their lives. How could he bear to be in this waiting room while she was only yards away fighting for her very life? How could someone else be making the most important decisions concerning her well-being? "O God, I hate you. Please help us."

The waiting, the hideous waiting, continued for two more days and nights. Then her eyes opened. They just opened as though awakening after a good night's sleep. She saw Pete sitting in the chair beside her bed looking twenty years older than she remembered. Her first word was both a question and a command, "Tommy?"

After another hour during which a thorough examination was hastily performed by a jubilant hospital staff, it became abundantly clear that if someone didn't produce Tom at Cooper's bedside all hell was going to break loose.

Tom's countenance was still one of grave concern until their eyes met and the explosion of relief that swept across his face became a cherished indelible memory for Cooper. "Where you been, Preppy? Out chasing nurses while I was in here trying to stay alive so's I could continue to complicate your life?"

"If you put so much as a dint in the woodie..." He couldn't do their thing under these circumstances. Taking her hand, he began to cry in spite of himself. They dissolved into that most intimate of silences and luxuriated in the sheer pleasure of once again being together in the flesh.

After a very long time Cooper broke the silence, "They told me that you weren't allowed in my room the whole time. It must have been awful for you."

"That will never happen again. As soon as we're married, I'll cold-cock the bastard that tries to come between me and my girl."

"What a perfectly charming proposal. That was a proposal of marriage was it not?"

With that they were off and running. How quickly despair can brighten into the glorious normalcy that too often we fail to appreciate and celebrate. As they say, life can, indeed, turn on a dime.

Epilogue

Cooper and Tom had agreed that while the "act" of marriage might have had very little to do with the commitment and spiritual union they had already found in each other, it definitely had advantages when living in the "real" world of laws, hospital rules, and other conventions which couples encounter at every turn.

Their marriage was truly celebrated by the entire cove community that seemed to take no small measure of credit for "getting them together." The actual ceremony was somewhat unorthodox in a number of ways, not the least of which was having the officiating priest as both best man and bride's man. Pete gave away his daughter and gained a devoted son. The act seemed to give him new life as he turned immediately to the task of plotting how he would finagle ways of getting his future grandbabies to himself.

The couple settled into the houseboat with Caroline and fell into a routine of fixing dinner each evening up at Pete's cottage. In time Caroline finally left the boat and followed them up the hill and sat in Pete's lap on the porch while Cooper and Tom did the dishes. Campy sat with them, of course, because no one ever really left the cove.

On one such evening, Tom had gone upstairs to the small marina office to capture a few ideas on Cooper's PC while she finished supper. On entering the room he found that the computer had been left on and, to his amazement, on the screen were the words **"IS ANY BODY THERE?"** Tom smiled, turned off the machine, and returned to the kitchen. He came up behind Cooper at the stove, put his arms around her and whispered in her ear, "yes."

THE END

We thought it an escape,
if only for a moment

Little did we realize,
suspended in time

Some part of us
had always been there

Some part would
always remain

About the Author

Vic Duggins lives in Knoxville, Tennessee with his wife, Gail, an intuitive consultant. They share four grown children by previous marriages. Two dogs, two cats and a menagerie of spirits also inhabit the Duggins home.

Vic enjoys hiking in the Great Smoky Mountains and boating on East Tennessee's beautiful lakes. His passions are focused on family, friends and intriguing strangers.